The Devil's Presence

a novel

James Oliver Goldsborough

City Point Press

Published by:
City Point Press
P.O. Box 2063
Westport, CT 06880
www.citypointpress.com

Paperback ISBN 978-1-947951-66-2
eBook ISBN 978-1-947951-67-9

Book and cover design by Alexia Garaventa
Manufactured in the United States of America

For the denizens of Playa del Rey,
those that are left.

"Simple folk never sense the devil's presence,

not even when his hands are on their throats."

—Mephistopheles in Auerbach's Leipzig wine-cellar:
Goethe: Faust, Part 1

"He who passively accepts evil is as much involved with it as he who helps to perpetrate it. He who accepts evil without protesting against it is really cooperating with it."

—Martin Luther King Jr.

Part One

Chapter 1

They knew the Kuhio Road as well as they knew the streets at home and were already tired of it. They walked it every morning, knew its churches, tiki bars and surf shops. After a late breakfast, they went to the beach for reading and swimming. It was early spring, and the water was far warmer than it would be at home. They'd come to the islands to escape. At home things were bad, and the islands seemed far enough away that they could forget about it. But they couldn't. At least he couldn't, couldn't get the misery out of his mind.

He watched her coming up from the bay, dripping, smiling, toweling off. They weren't young anymore, but she still looked good. That had never been a problem.

"If the water was like this at home, I'd swim every day," she said.

"Probably twenty degrees difference in water temperature."

"So why don't we move here?"

She was kidding. She would never leave her friends.

"We don't want to look for new doctors," he said.

Later, they walked back to the house they'd rented off Weke Road. The first thing he'd done after arrival was to unplug the television. He couldn't keep her from using her devices, but she was getting better at leaving them off. Limit the bad news. That's why they'd come. Recharge. Try for a new start.

He'd had a good swim out beyond the surf, close to a half-mile, he figured. He felt it. The frustrating thing about growing old is that you can be in as good shape as ever but the body knows the difference and likes reminding you. Too many dead cells. Stamina isn't what it was. He'd been swimming every day since they arrived, managing by the third time out to put sharks out of his mind. There'd been an attack in the bay. A girl lost an arm. He'd been warned.

Home from the beach in mid-afternoon, he ate a few crackers, drank some pineapple juice and headed for the shower. Dried off, feeling good from the swim as always, he drew the curtains and stretched out on the bed to read a chapter in his Simenon novel and maybe fall asleep. The house had three bedrooms, but they only used two. Nancy would nap in her own room. She took a nap every day. He only napped when he needed to, which was more often than it used to be.

The first thing he'd wanted to know about the house was the bedrooms. There had to be at least two, and they—or at least his—had to have curtains, not sheers or blinds or shades, but real curtains. He needed dark to sleep, day or night, dark and quiet, always had. Nancy was the opposite, needed fresh air and didn't mind light. The house on Weke looked north toward Hanalei Bay, but the bedrooms faced east. When the sun came up over the Princeville hills it shone bright into the bedrooms. The owners, a Japanese couple on the south side of the island who came to Hanalei only in summer, knew about the sun. They'd put in good curtains, thick and opaque. They'd sent photos.

That night they walked to Sam's on Kuhio for grilled opa and drinks. Nancy had cooked when they first arrived, but gave it up when they discovered Sam's. It was an island place like most with thatch and bamboo and nets with shells on the wall, but it had its pretensions. The food and coconut rum drinks were good and for dinner you had to have shoes and a shirt to get seated, which kept out the surfers. Masks were required, but you took them off when seated. Laid-back Kauai wasn't Oahu, and rural Hanalei wasn't Honolulu, not even Lihue. The fish at Sam's was fresh, and the only music was an old Hawaiian who sat in a corner with his ukulele singing about the humuhumu-nukunukuapia'a that went swimming by. Turned out to be a triggerfish, said Sam, who was Japanese/American, advising him to stick with the opa. The waitresses wore print sarongs and looked good in them. Nancy said sarongs were good for women of a certain age.

"How come we don't eat this at home?" he asked.

"Not sure. I've never seen opa at the pier."

"Must be a warm water fish."

"We have swordfish."

He stirred some mint leaves in his Hawaiian mojito. "Swordfish is good. Especially the way you do it."

"I don't want to set you off," she said after a moment, "but the news from home is really awful."

"I thought you were going to leave those things turned off."

"You can't remove yourself from the world."

"So what awful news are you referring to?"

"The fires."

"Ah, the fires."

"We may not have a state to return to."

"Our own fault."

She stared at him. "What do you mean?"

"I mean too many people just don't give a damn. We'll be dead anyway, they say, so why worry about the planet? Let it burn."

She frowned and sipped her mojito. "The pandemic is spreading. Millions will die, they say now. Worse than the Black Plague."

"At least."

"Trump says it's fake," she said.

"Millions dead is fake?"

"Riots in Portland, Chicago, Philadelphia and Louisville."

"Louisville?"

"Police shot a woman in her apartment. Andy, I don't get it. Okay, so we're not all alike. That doesn't mean we have to kill each other. They don't do that in other countries."

"Slavery," he said. "Americans can't get past it."

"You think that's what it is?"

"Trump legitimizes their hate."

"Whose hate?"

"The supremacists."

She didn't answer, and he fished for a mint leaf. "You know, there was a time when all the bad news wasn't about America. When I worked for the Paris paper sometimes the front page would have nothing from the States. Everything was crisis in Berlin or Cuba or China or the Middle East. Trouble in South Africa was big. Indonesia. We had Vietnam, but in Europe that wasn't big news."

"Front page news has to be bad, doesn't it?"

"Mostly."

They walked home along dark and empty streets. Kuhio went to bed early in the time of the plagues.

The old question: Does how you feel determine how you see the news, or does the news determine how you feel? The idea that we'd passed the tipping point was upon him each day, his first conscious thought of the morning. It wasn't always like that. He remembered days when he would awaken with zest for the new day. "When the sun comes up the whole world dances with joy and everyone's heart is filled with bliss," roshi Suzuki wrote somewhere. Not anymore. The idea of bliss and dancing with joy belonged to some other world.

He'd grown estranged from his friends and even from his wife, which is why they'd come to Hanalei. At home, they'd tried avoiding reality for months, but after a while it didn't work anymore. At least, for him, it didn't. The ship was heading for the rocks with an idiot at the helm, and he had to sound the alarm. His friends eventually stopped listening. They were sick of him but too civilized to argue all the time. So they dropped him.

It was hard on Nancy. She still played tennis and had her bridge group and backyard parties. Only now she went without him. The Trump venom had leaked into his own marriage. That's when he thought of the islands, of getting away, try a little escape. Maybe the planet was dying, viruses running rampant and government run by liars and grifters, but you still had your life to live. Her friends called him paranoid and told her not to listen to his rants. Some were going to vote for Trump, she told him; it's their right. That's when he first suspected. No, he said, it's nobody's right to support the devil. He couldn't sit at a table, even stay in the room with those people. They were the enablers, the comforters, the amen chorus. The thought that voters would return to power in November the perpetrators of their own destruction was too much for him. But Nancy?

He'd brought her to Kauai years before on their honeymoon so why not try again? Maybe Hanalei was part of the dying world, but it didn't seem to be. Tucked away on the empty north coast of a small island lost in the middle of a great ocean, cooled by winds from the west, it seemed immune. He would turn off the news, exorcise fire, disease, death, and the devil from his consciousness and start breathing again. Nancy, too.

It didn't work. Ten days away, and she wanted to get back to her routines. They found it hard to talk and just as hard to stay silent. Their minds had entered different orbits.

Incompatibility? After thirty-five years marriage? But they'd always been compatible. That's why they married. They'd both reached age forty with full lives and no intention of giving up independence. Then they met and decided to give it up. Nancy had always had men around her, but never one she wanted to marry. That's what she told him. For him— except for the French girl he'd married and the English girl who came between them—it was the same.

He'd met Nancy in the lingerie department of Robinson's in Beverly Hills. She helped him find the negligee he wanted, and he couldn't stop thinking how it would look on her. She wrote her name on the sales receipt, and when he brought it back she didn't seem surprised.

"The wrong size? She didn't like it? But it's so pretty."

"I gave her something else."

They started dating soon afterward. When they married six months later in the Lutheran Church on Wilshire most of the guests were her friends. He was working at the *Times* in those days and invited a few friends, mostly from the newspaper. Her friends were from everywhere, some from Robinson's, some from church, some from when she'd arrived in the city from Milwaukee twenty years earlier and even a few from back home. She was a popular and attractive girl, as much with men as with women. There'd been some men who wanted to marry her, but she wasn't ready.

Some of them, she confessed, were already married. One of her friends said she was attracted to married men precisely because they weren't available. She saw the truth in it. You had to be available in case something better came along. For some reason she regarded Andy McKnight as something better. Maybe he was in those days.

Nancy Neefe had come to town in the sixties with a girlfriend, both of them dropping out of a Wisconsin community college. They were good German girls from good Lutheran farm families—Nancy's family claimed a distant relationship to Christian Gottlob Neefe, Beethoven's first music teacher, though no one in her Wisconsin family was musical. Nancy was the first in the family to leave the farm, but she had more on her mind than becoming a farmer's wife. Too much work, too many children, too little hope. She had no Hollywood aspirations, but had seen brochures on Southern California, so that's where they headed. She found a sales job at Robinson's, an apartment with her friend in Santa Monica and only returned to the farm for weddings and funerals.

The trip home from Kauai was gloomy. He'd plugged in the television the last day to see what he'd missed. Trump was doubling down as elections approached, tormenting the nation as long as he could. What strange psychosis causes a man to regard the earth and humanity as enemies? What strange psychoticism infects a nation that elects such a creature? The fires still raged, the temperatures still climbed, the plague still spread, businesses still shut down, Trump still lied and denied and insulted. No country wanted anything to do with the United States anymore. Trump banned Europeans, and Europeans banned Americans. We were isolated. Kim and Putin, the dictators, were our friends now.

Kim and Putin, bloodthirsty Stalinists longing for the good old days. Trump thought he could do business with them. What kind of fool was he?

The flight was smooth, passengers masked and scattered. Honolulu airport was almost empty; few flights to the islands these days. She kept on her earphones, he read his novel. He'd almost bought a *New York Times* when they changed planes from Lihue but didn't want any more bad news. He wasn't sure how much worse things could get, but anything was possible with a bomb-thrower. He thought of the *New Yorker* cartoon he'd put on the refrigerator four years before. A man in bed tells his bedmate, who is setting the alarm, "wake me in 2020."

The alarm was ringing.

LAX was bad, the airport a massive construction zone as the city tried to undo the self-inflicted damage of a few decades before when it pulled up eleven hundred miles of rails and trolleys—called by some the world's best urban transit system—to replace them with cars, highways, and carbon dioxide. At the cost of countless billions, it was now rebuilding the trolley system in an attempt to get rid of cars, highways, and carbon dioxide. He'd edited a story for the *Times* about that, the author pointing out that the new system would precisely follow the lines of the old system, a demonstration, said the writer, that the human race was not getting smarter, as evolutionists once predicted.

Smoke from fires in the mountains was as strong as when they'd left. It took a half hour to find a taxi and another twenty minutes to get out of the airport. He told the driver to skip the freeway and take Lincoln Boulevard. They lived on 22nd Street in Santa Monica, a street far west of the freeway so no use getting stuck in freeway traffic. They'd just started the freeway system when he was at UCLA, and he remembered the transportation professor explaining that it would never work. Freeways would simply attract more drivers until they were as slow as the surface streets. What then?

Turning off Lincoln a half hour later, he saw people wearing masks along Wilshire. Nancy had bought masks in a shop on Kuhio, hand-made by native Hawaiians, they said. The driver turned again onto 22nd, a few more leafy blocks to go. They passed the former house of Jack Ferraro, one person he'd always looked forward to seeing. "For Sale" was still up on the lawn. The Ferraros had moved to New Zealand to escape fires, smoke, and the plagues. Escape America. It was a slow real estate market, and their house hadn't yet sold. Retired people needed $1 million each to emigrate to New Zealand to cover the costs of the health care system, which was free. Jack had saved a million and borrowed the rest against his house.

Buck up, he told himself as they approached their house; nobody who lives on a street like this in a town like this has a right to complain. Think of the people who don't have something like this to return to, who don't have anything to return to. Think of the people who have been burnt out, lost their loved ones, their jobs, their business, their hopes, their dreams, their lives. He tried that line of thought the rest of the way home. It didn't stick.

Chapter 2

He hadn't checked his messages in a month and was in no hurry to do so. There'd been a time when he checked constantly, afraid of missing something. The life of a newspaperman. Lately, he didn't care what he missed, since all the news was bad. Opening the suitcases while Nancy drove to the market on Montana, he decided email could wait another day. He could have checked it on Kauai, but liked the idea of going to ground. If people needed to reach him (unlikely, he knew), his messages would have gone through Nancy's account. There was also the possibility that he would have no messages, another reason not to check. If he'd had any reason to expect good news, he'd have gone straight to the computer.

Needing exercise to restore him, he changed into shorts and a T-shirt and set out up Carlyle toward the country club, a familiar route. In the old days, he might have dropped in for a friendly cocktail with the boys at the bar, but he didn't go to the club anymore, didn't even know if the bar was open during the plague. They'd joined soon after they married when initiation fees were still four figures, not six. Nancy played tennis and joined the bridge group. He'd done some swimming and played tennis, but was still at the *Times* in those days and didn't have much free time. He discovered he didn't like club people, whose principal interest was golf and their portfolios. For swimming, he preferred the ocean anyway.

He'd made the walk along Carlyle, up to 25th, around to Georgina and home again hundreds of times, but never tired of it. He liked his neighborhood, and a good half-hour on the streets generally pulled him out of whatever sour mood had gotten into him. Carlyle was good for walking, sheltered in thick pines instead of the palms on most Santa Monica streets, easier to breathe, maybe because evergreens absorbed more smoke from the fires in the foothills. The street lighting was just right, tall dewdrop lampposts hidden by taller trees that did not give off too much light. He liked the dark.

Nancy was home when he got back, and they made ham and cheese sandwiches for dinner. She made a salad. He opened a bottle of pinot noir from the days before Napa burnt down. He could see she was happy to be home.

"You check your messages?" she asked.

"Tomorrow."

"Phone?"

"Mostly robocalls."

"Our surface mail should resume tomorrow."

"You have anything planned?"

"Call around, see what the girls are doing. How about you?"

"Might drive down to the beach."

"Twenty degrees difference, that what you said?"

"I may not last a half mile."

"No sharks, though."

He laughed.

"It's good to see you laugh."

He sipped his wine. "I can't find much to laugh about."

"You have to try harder."

After breakfast the following day, with Nancy off to the club to see what she'd missed, he went into his den, shut the door, and turned on the computer. He'd shut it down and had to log on, looking up the password he could never remember. He had a good many messages, mostly junk, and scanned quickly. Then he looked again, closer this time, his eyes stopping on a name he'd ignored the first time. The name was Philippa. There was a message from someone named Philippa Hughes. Philippa, meaning "lover of horses," is a rare woman's name, a fact he knew from years before.

He stared at the name a while before opening it. He'd known a Philippa Grey, an English girl who worked at the British Hospital in Paris. He had fallen in love with that Philippa, and his mind went to her, though his fingers still did not open the message. Was it even possible? He'd often thought of Philippa, whom he'd lost when he left Paris. He remembered their last night at her flat on the Avenue Niel. After that, he'd gone to New York on a six-month transfer, and when he returned to Paris, she was gone. He called the hospital. Nurse Grey no longer worked at the hospital, they said. She had returned to England.

He was daydreaming, his mind back fifty years, roaming the streets of Paris, Left Bank places in Saint-Germain and Montparnasse, but mostly Right Bank. They both lived and worked on the Right Bank, and their haunts were places like Vattier's, Fouquet's and Val d'Isère. And Churchill's. Never forget Churchill's. Still he did not open the message. Was it her? Did he want it to be her, an old woman now? For him, Philippa Grey was forever twenty-five and beautiful and sexy and in love with him. And Paris, of course. It could be her. He was published enough that he was not hard to find, but why now? Why after so many years? Would this be another sad story of what might have been, flights of memory like in Proust and Modiano? A newspaperman forever attached to the present, he didn't like that kind of story.

He was being silly. More women are named Philippa than Philippa Grey.

He clicked open.

Dear Andy,

> *I hope this gets to you. I found one of your books in a used bookshop in Plymouth and looked you up. Why not? Do you even remember me, I wonder? I liked the book about Paris very much. I hope you are well in these terrible times. I'd love to hear from you. I came back to Devon after you left for New York. So long ago.*

> *Philippa*

> *p.s. You'll notice that I have a different family name now. I did get married.*

> *P.*

He sat frozen for some time, though his mind was anything but frozen. Churchill's off the Champs Élysées was where he'd met her. He was at the bar one night nursing a Canadian Club. It was after eleven and he'd left the newspaper on rue de Berri after the first edition and wasn't ready to go home to a wife that wasn't there. She'd come in with a group of Brits that pushed two tables together and were making too much noise. He watched them in the mirror and immediately noticed her because she was so pretty and didn't seem like the others, was a little darker, a little quieter, didn't have a *serieux* in front of her, one of those giant glasses of tap beer that make you pee all night. He ordered another Canadian and watched.

There were eight of them, five men, three women, all but her with a *serieux*. She was drinking white wine. Lovely red lips, shy smile, dark hair curled over her head, quietly enjoying the company but not joining in the fun. A little embarrassed, maybe. The English have a bad reputation in Paris from the rugby league, tend to go on rampages after games, tear things up, especially on the Champs Élysées, near Churchill's.

He was a semi-regular at Churchill's on nights he worked late and didn't want to go home, but hadn't seen this group before. Ian, the Scots bartender, saw him watching in the mirror. "Docs and nurses from the British Hospital. Tend to come by after a hard night."

"Not like the rugby crowd."

"Those are the English. This is a mixed group. Two of the docs are Scots, one's Irish, even a Welshman. Good people. Save your life."

"You know anything about the dark-haired girl?"

"Ah, the pretty one. Doesn't talk much. I think she's English. You want to meet her?"

"Now how am I going to do that?"

"You're a newspaper guy. Tell them you want to do a story on the British Hospital. I bet you didn't even know there was a British Hospital in Paris."

"As matter of fact ..."

"There you are. Want me to go over?"

It worked out better than he had any reason to hope. Ian went over, and the next thing he knew they were waving him over.

"*Herald Tribune*," said a doc with a Scots accent, "and you don't know about the British Hospital in Paris? For shame. Bloody place has been there for a century. Much longer than the American Hospital. I'm Mac," he said, extending his hand. "These are my buddies, left to right, Carol, Colin, Tommy, Emma, Titty, Simon, and Phil. Pull up a chair."

He pulled up his chair between Simon and Phil, two BHP nurses, male and female. Simon was the Welshman. When they left an hour later he had a name, a hospital address, information that her real name was Philippa, that she hated being called Phil but the doctors wouldn't stop. There was a smile for him before she was packed into a waiting Citroen with Titty, whose real name was Titus and who was the lead surgeon at the hospital in spite of his name, at the wheel.

Nancy was home from the club with the news that they'd been invited to dinner by Susan and Joe Godfrey if they would get virus tests first. He was surprised. Nancy and Susan were tennis and bridge friends from the club, but it had been a long time since he'd seen Joe.

"Will you go?" she asked.

"The Godfreys?"

"Susan is one of my best friends. She wants you to see their new house."

"They're not serious about getting tests."

"Oh, yes they are, and they're right. We've been away a month, been in airports, taxis and planes."

"We were tested at the airports, coming and going."

"One more won't hurt. We don't want to wear masks at dinner. Will you go?"

Yes, he would go. He owed it to her.

The Godfreys used to live on 17th Street, around a couple of corners from Carlyle. At the time, Joe was scrounging out a living at the studios doing rewrite work, more or less the same stuff Andy was doing for the *Times*. They became tennis pals until Joe moved into a bigger and better job and into a bigger and better house in Mandeville Canyon. Nancy described the house as "palatial." She'd been there a few times for bridge.

Dinner was the following Thursday. The Godfreys lived on a cul de sac in the Santa Monica Mountains that you wouldn't find unless you had the address, a map, and a flashlight. Mandeville is across Sunset and straight up through rows of sycamores, pines, and eucalyptus, trees so high, thick and old you don't always know there are houses under them. The city's glitterati love the canyons, which stretch into the mountains on dozens of winding roads between the ocean and Hollywood. The canyons are best visited by day for the streets are narrow and unlighted with house numbers invisible for a reason. No drop-ins, please. By daylight you still see traces of the Mandeville fire that raged through the area a few years back, bringing down hundreds of homes and causing people to swear never to build again in the mountains. Despite fire insurance as expensive as mortgages, they came back. Money does that. They'd been lucky since then; the fires had been in other places: the Simi fire, the Getty fire, the Mureau fire, the Dexter fire, the Brea fire, the Easy fire, on and on, hardly a canyon untouched. You want a job in L.A.? Become a firefighter or an insurance adjuster.

Kimberly Lane was not more than four miles from Carlyle Avenue, but was straight up and belonged to a different world. Driving up, he felt conflicted. For Nancy's sake he couldn't refuse, but dinner invitations in these awful times seemed grotesque. She pleaded with him to have a few drinks, loosen up and for God's sake stay off the gloom and doom. She knew the way, recognized the house from the lane with its Spanish turrets and towers. It was the kind of place built by the movie moguls in the thirties and meticulously maintained. The Mandeville fire had been just to the east. It had brought canyon prices down. Then they went back up.

Susan was at the door with Joe just behind. Neither wore masks. She greeted them from behind the screen door with, "you've both been tested, I trust." Nancy nodded, and Susan opened the door. She was a small woman, nearly Nancy's age, and surgery had only helped for a while. The women embraced, and Joe clapped him on the shoulder. "Been a while, Andy. Glad you could make it. Nancy, let me take your jacket."

He was a tall man with a soft face that hid a hard mind. He'd added serious poundage to his once lanky frame. Despite the wives' friendship, Andy hadn't seen Joe in a few years, since he'd been promoted to studio "script doctor," and they'd moved to the canyon. He'd joined a club nearer his Burbank studio. Paying for two country clubs plus a mortgage on a $5 million house was not something ordinary people did, but doctoring scripts is more than newspaper rewrite work. A difference of a million annually. Or maybe two. Or three.

Sunk deep into plush cushions on heavy oak furniture, they took drinks with a fire blazing across a cozy living room. Cooler up in the mountains. Listening to the chitchat, Andy found himself thinking about embers landing on the dry pines outside, wondering if they had a fire screen on the chimney. Nancy inquired about the children.

"They're still in Denver. Won't get on a plane until this is over."

"We did," Andy said.

Susan frowned. "So tell us about it. It's been ages since we've been to Kauai."

Over cheese and prosciutto hors d'oeuvres and a Saratoga Chardonnay, the women did most of the talking and the men most of the drinking. Joe told him about movie troubles. Nobody went to theaters anymore, but demand for television and streaming scripts had never been stronger, everything tailored to the new stay-at-home world.

"You think theaters will come back?" Andy asked.

"No. But who needs them?"

"Depends if you like getting out of the house."

"My life is home to club and shopping and back again," said Susan. "Speaking of that, Andy, I haven't seen you at the club in ages. Your wife could use a partner, you know."

She couldn't resist. It was a sore spot.

"For what?" he asked.

"All the games we play. Games help us get through this, you know."

In the dining room, Joe uncorked a 2012 Sterling cabernet to go with Susan's roast beef. He had a temperature-controlled wine unit in his garage and took periodic trips into the California wine country to stock it.

"Enjoy it while you can," he said. "Sterling went up in the fires."

"Four percent of the state lost," said Andy.

"Things will get better," Joe said, passing plates around.

How easily talk slipped into the miseries of the present. Conversation was like sluicing down a giant funnel: start anywhere and you end up in the same narrow hole. The comment annoyed him, but he responded gently: "You sure about that, Joe?"

"Hey," cried Susan, "you checked your portfolio lately? We call it our Trump portfolio."

Too much, and he felt Nancy's pleading eyes on him. Susan was one of those bringing us closer to the black hole. Maybe they all would, though he'd read that white suburban women had soured on the man. But what about rich, white, Mandeville Canyon suburban women with big houses and big portfolios? Susan infected Nancy, he knew she did.

He turned to the hostess. Since he was asked, he ought to reply.

"I hope you are using your portfolio money to help get this contemptible jackass out of the White House before it is too late."

He'd told himself to go slowly, that these were Nancy's friends and she needed them even if he didn't, but the wine was good and he was beyond the point of hiding his feelings, even of editing them into socially acceptable form. These were dangerous times. He didn't like being quarrelsome in someone else's home, but Susan's portfolio comment had cut deep. What did a little more paper money mean on a planet going down?

No one responded. Frowning again, Susan stared at him, looked to her husband, to Nancy, then back to Andy. "He's the president, you know."

He started to reply and stopped. He would say neither what she wanted nor what he was thinking.

Susan waited, shook her head, stood and silently began clearing plates away. He quickly finished his last piece of roast beef, which was prime cut. He wondered why she didn't have a maid, though maybe Thursday was the maid's day off. Nancy rose to help, leaving the men alone at the table, staring at right angles to each other. He glanced at the 2012 Sterling cabernet bottle. It was empty.

"I don't think Susan appreciated your jackass comment," Joe said after a moment.

Andy turned to him. "How about you?"

"Vulgar."

"Like the man himself."

"Which man would that be?"

They belonged to different clubs now, different worlds. Joe stood. Andy stood. Silence. They listened to whispering voices from the kitchen. "Let's go into the living room and wait for the women," Joe said. "Susan will bring coffee."

Only she didn't. When the women came out, Nancy announced it was time to go, and Joe went to the closet for her jacket. Nancy and Susan were embracing. "See you at the club," Susan said to Nancy. The men shook hands.

They didn't talk on the short ride home. He couldn't think of anything that wouldn't sound inane. Nancy was steaming but didn't say a word, hated confrontations. When she was mad, she sometimes muttered things under her breath, but when she was really steaming she went mute, leaving him to imagine the worst.

He should have refused the invitation. She'd expected him to return from the islands with all the anger and vexation out of his system, ready to pick up where they once were: a happily married couple with old friends and social responsibilities. He couldn't do it. The sensitive feelings of his wife and her friends didn't balance against a nation gone mad and a world in mortal peril.

Someone had to speak up. He thought of *Network*, great old movie where the angry news anchor starts ranting on air: "I'm mad as hell and I'm not going to take it anymore." Soon he has people across the country flinging open their windows and shouting along with him.

That's what Andy wanted: Everybody screaming out their rage until Trump slunk back into his hole.

Chapter 3

Dear Philippa,

Is it really you? Are you the Philippa Grey I knew in Paris? If you knew how often I've thought of you, wondered what you'd become, wondered if you were even alive. I called the hospital when I returned from New York, and they said you'd gone. Gone where, I asked? Back to England, they said. I got Simon on the phone. You'd promised to send him an address. Nothing came. You'd left no trail. On purpose, Simon told me. Don't try to find her; she doesn't want to see you, doesn't want to come back. I was desolate. I didn't understand.

I didn't understand until I'd left Paris myself. Until you're gone, you don't understand that you can't leave Paris. You say it's over and you go back to London or New York or wherever and try to move on. You purge everything to get on with your life. I tried the same thing when I returned to California but kept being pulled back. Couldn't shake it. Couldn't forget anything about Paris or about you—your name, your face, our days, our nights. Someone wrote that we reinvent the world each time we remember. Why shouldn't we in a world like we have today?

Lovely to hear from you after so long. You returned to Devon, to your origins, back to the be-

ginning, just like me. Married and with how many
children? And grandchildren? I hope life has been
good to you. You deserve it. How many people re-
connect after a half century? Paris does things like
that. Write back and tell me everything.

    Andy

His French marriage had worked well enough for a while,
though they were both young and soon wondering what
they'd done. Claire was twenty-one, already a rebel of sorts,
tired of living at home and dating French boys, whom she
said all "wear a dirty sweater, smoke a Gaulois and think
they have the right to sleep with you on the first date." She
called it the *"droit du seigneur"* and hated it. She liked the
idea of scandalizing her very bourgeois family by marrying
a foreigner who worked at the *Paris Herald* and was called a
journaliste, a glamorous profession in those days.

As for Andy McKnight, he was twenty-five, had landed in
Paris almost by accident, and after a rocky few weeks on the
job sensed he would be there for a while. Working nights, he
had little time for dating, so when he found a French girl who
was pretty, available, spoke some English and didn't sleep with
him on the first date, he was ready. It only started to go wrong
when she inherited a farmhouse in Normandy, near Anet, and
decided she was a country girl. It came down to the farmhouse
or him, and it was an easier choice for her than it should have
been. One night, not wanting to go home to an empty flat after
work, he dropped into Churchill's off the Champs Élysées and
met an English girl who changed everything.

Nancy was already up and gone when he came down the
next morning, a rare event and a sign she'd not slept well. She

didn't come back until late that night, walked by the living room where he was reading and went to her room without a word. The next morning, she did not come down at all. The ice had settled thick and strong over the McKnight household. After breakfast, he went to his computer.

Dear Andy,

I was so angry. You left without even saying goodbye. You abandoned me. Why, oh why? I wondered. I stayed on in Paris a bit after that, but it wasn't in me anymore. They wanted to send me to nurse's school, but I was never keen on that. Too queasy, you know. I went home for a while, and my mother asked if I was pregnant. Imagine! No, you can't. You'd have to be a woman. I wasn't pregnant, I was simply miserable with my life. Paris is a wonderful place to be young and in love, but an absolutely horrible place to be lonely. It's no wonder people keep throwing themselves into the Seine. "The abyss, the abyss," wrote Baudelaire, who was always alone, except for his mother, who wasn't much help.

I started back with the doc to try to forget you— the doc at the American Hospital if you remember— but it was a mistake. I was in love, and you were gone. Oh, I can't say I didn't expect it someday. You never hid from me that you were married, and I accepted it. But just to up and go without a goodbye? And after that last night! Did you know then? You wrote a few letters from New York that I kept for years before finally ripping them up. I wish I'd kept them now. I began work in a bookstore and met a fine man. I was happy with Dennis and happy to have two wonderful children and then three won-derful grandchildren. Dennis died two years ago, and the children and grandchildren moved away. I see them sometimes, but not enough.

When Dennis died I went back to the bookstore to help out when they were short. And one day I came upon a book of yours. I found your address and wrote, hardly thinking it would arrive or that you would answer. You're right. It's been half a cen-tury! How strange it is to write something like that, to think we're that old and it's been that long. Write and tell me what's become of you. I hope you were just a little put out when you returned and found I was gone.

Philippa

The following morning he was in the kitchen when she came down, a sign perhaps of a thaw setting in. She was still in her robe, which was unusual. He'd intended to walk before breakfast, but put it off. They hadn't said two words since returning from dinner at the Godfreys. They exchanged good mornings, their first two words; he went outside for the newspaper and came back to heat the wa-ter, grind the coffee and put it in the French press to brew, things he'd done thousands of times. He sensed that cof-fee wasn't the only thing brewing. Silently, she put plates and cups on the kitchen table and set out milk, butter and jam. She cut up an apple and brought out the baguette he'd bought at the bakery on Montana. When the coffee was ready, he pressed and poured. Neither took sugar, though he took a little milk. Their kitchen faced east, so they already had sunlight filtering through the smoke and the pines. When it got a little higher, he would run down the blinds. He wanted to talk, but nothing came out. Except for the silence, everything seemed as always.

He glanced at her as she sipped her coffee. She looked tired. Their eyes met, and she started to say something, but what came out was a long sigh. "Ah, Andy."

He held his cup in both hands, feeling its warmth.

"Something is happening to us," she said.

"Not just to us."

"I don't mean that. I mean just to us."

"Inevitable."

"Your one-word answers don't help much."

He nodded, took a sip, waited for the coffee to clear his mind. "I think the answer is that for the first time in my life I feel absolutely helpless. I don't know what to do. I am lost and I am searching."

It didn't resonate. "Why does that make you different from anyone else?" she insisted. "We're all in this together."

"I wish we were."

"Why do you feel so alone?"

"Because of all the Susan Godfreys, I guess."

Her face flushed. "What you said in her house the other night was disgraceful. Susan was furious. She'll never have us back again."

"*Us?*"

She stared at him until he had to look away.

"You're saying that I can go alone? That I can do everything alone, like during these past few days? What's come over you, Andy? You didn't use to be like this."

"I can't see people like Susan Godfrey anymore."

"Susan is my friend."

"Susan is the problem."

"Are you sure that you're not the problem?"

They were glaring at each other. "I am not the problem. I am the solution. If there is one, that is."

"How?"

"I don't know."

"It's like you're sick, like you've caught something. Some of my friends think ..."

"What?"

Her face softened for the first time. "Dementia?"

It was almost funny. "I'd love to escape into a little dementia. Or drugs. It shouldn't be hard to find a little leftover acid in Santa Monica."

She focused hard on him. "Frivolity doesn't help."

"What would you suggest?"

"I don't know. At our age, solutions aren't easy. If this were something normal—an accident, an affair, yes, even dementia, I'd know what to do. I've always known what to do, you know that. But this—what is it, anyway, existential angst, one of my friends calls it. How do you treat something like that?"

"Which friend would that be?"

"What does it matter? It's just that everyone thinks you're going crazy."

He gazed at her for a long time, this woman he had loved for so many years, forever it seemed, so much longer than with any other woman. She was a good woman—attractive, clever, generous, loving. But something was changing.

"I may be the last sane one."

"That's what the inmates in the asylums say."

"Maybe they're right."

"I don't know any more when you're serious and when you're joking."

"This is no joke."

"So you're going to parade around town with a sign saying, 'repent, the end is near,' like those religious crazies. You're not even religious."

He couldn't make her understand, couldn't make anyone understand. "I have to do something, don't you see?" He felt his voice rising. "I can't sit around anymore listening to people like Susan Godfrey in their castles telling me, hey, maybe the fires are raging and glaciers melting and the seas rising but don't worry because just look at our portfolios. Don't worry about a crazy president doing crazy things because we're all getting rich."

Her face was tight. "Susan's a good person. Stop picking on her."

"She stands for all the others I can't pick on."

"There are thousands of people working for the environment, you know."

"We've sent them money for years, and what good has it done? It's too late. The Trumps, the Kochs, Murdoch and Fox News, the crooks and the cronies, the oil lobbyists who run the EPA, the Susan Godfreys have won. They have contaminated everything with their money and their lies—including government and the law. We have lost."

"How dare you put her in there with those others? What has she done?"

"She supports them. She enables them."

Neither had touched the food. Coffee, yes, that's what coffee is for, to shock the system, to get the little gray cells working again, to find solutions.

"I used to think of you as brave, Andy, a man standing up to the evils of the world. That's the kind of writer you were. But that's not how people see you now. They see you as eccentric ... or worse, a crank. What good does it do to save the world if you bring your own world tumbling down around you? That's not bravery, that's insanity. Those people are called paranoids and are locked up to protect themselves—and others."

"Paranoids worry about imaginary enemies. Is it paranoid to see disease all around us; to see the air, water and land permanently fouled under mankind's accumulating filth? Is it paranoid to see a man in the White House who has corrupted an entire nation? Look what those people are doing to us!"

"*Those people!* Aren't you one of us? Aren't you an American?"

Finally, his voice dropped. "I am not one of those people. No."

Then: "Are you?"

She turned toward the windows, looking toward a backyard growing ratty under water restrictions. The pines in the foothills still held their own. Pines are survivors, manage to live hundreds of years—unless the forest fires get them. He followed her gaze up above the trees, up where the sky once was blue and clear. What wouldn't they give for some rainclouds to wash the smoke away. But the only dark clouds were inside.

She turned back. "I don't want this to end badly, Andy. I'm a little old for that. So are you. But we are right on the edge. Or let's say, I am right on the edge."

She stared at him until he had to look away. Yes, he saw it now. It had happened in his own house. Susan and the country club crowd had claimed her, too. Finally she looked away. How sad it was. Something in him wanted to throw his arms around this woman that he had loved for so long, return to what had always been. But there was no going back. They were in a new place.

She left for the club, and he left on his walk. Restless, conflicted, he chose a longer route, one that took him down to 14th, across to San Vicente and back up again, cutting in and out and across north-south streets that he rarely saw, giving himself more time to think, though his thoughts drifted, refused to focus. He glanced at the elegant houses behind the trees, behind the well-kept lawns. Into how many of those houses had the Trump poison seeped? How many kitchen scenes like his own were taking place? His life was coming apart, that was clear enough, but how many others? Walking always helped, especially city walking. Paris was the best for walking, so many varieties of people, shops, buildings, history on every corner. He'd covered hundreds of square miles in Paris in his time, every day coming upon some new little *passage* or *allée* with plaques on the buildings to show who was born or died there and maybe bullet holes in the stones to show who had been shot.

Lost in a miasma of dull thoughts, wearing a mask against smoke and virus, hardly paying attention to where he was, he looked up and found himself on lower Georgina, a handsome street under tall ficus trees lined with stately houses on both sides. Sometimes the only people he saw on his walks were the Japanese and Mexican gardeners who tended the grounds. They'd used leaf blowers until the city banned them for being loud and useless nuisances, blowing leaves from one house to another, street to sidewalk and back again. Some days, except for crossing an occasional matron with her yappy little dogs, he didn't see anyone.

Crossing 18ᵗʰ, he spied a strange man on the far side of Georgina, moving slowly, eyes fixed on the ground, long bag looped over a shoulder like Johnny Appleseed, carrying some kind of stick or cane. He slowed his pace and looked closer. The stick or cane was some kind of gripper tool, and the man was picking up trash. He wasn't dressed like a city sanitation worker but wore ordinary jeans and a gray sweater. He had a red bandana over his face and a floppy hat against the sun. Of more than a certain age, he wore rimless spectacles of the kind that darken with the sun. Andy nodded, but the man, fixated on a plastic bottle in the gutter, didn't notice. He'd never noticed that much trash on these streets, but the man's bag looked nearly full. He crossed over.

"What do you do when the bag's full?"

Surprised, maybe annoyed, he looked up, blinking against the sunlight, adjusting the bag. "I head for the trash cans."

"Where are the trash cans?"

He fixed Andy with his gaze. "San Vicente, Montana and Wilshire."

"I've never noticed much trash on these streets."

Narrowed eyes. "Maybe that's because I've been over them."

"How come I've never seen you before?"

"Lots of streets."

"I'm impressed."

Hesitation. Then: "What's to be impressed about?"

"Just that I've never seen anyone doing it before."

"Maybe I'm the only one."

"Why?"

"Somebody has to. "

"I've never seen it done before."

No answer.

"Why are you the only one?"

"Why all the questions?"

"It's a good thing you're doing."

"I suppose it is," he said, giving his bag a hitch. "Thank you." He started to move on, but stopped and turned. "You want to join me?"

Andy laughed. "I don't have a picker."

Sun glanced off the man's spectacles. "I'll bring you one."

"Not enough trash for two."

"I know some places."

"You're serious, aren't you?"

"Are you?"

"Say, what's your name?"

"Call me Max."

Chapter 4

Dear Philippa,

It was the other way around. I thought you had abandoned me. When I returned to Paris from New York my marriage was over. You ask if I was "put out" that you were gone. I was devastated, everything collapsed around me, personally and professionally. I was worthless to the newspaper, kept on thanks only to the editor, old Artie, who'd been through things like that himself. "You'll pull out of it, Andy," he said, "but try to hurry up, will you?" Got us both laughing. How different things might have been if you had stayed. We never thought ahead, did we? Too wrapped up in the moment. I didn't talk about my marriage, and you didn't hint that you wouldn't wait. But what a joy it was while it lasted. Memories forever.

It worked out for you, didn't it? Back to your roots to meet a good man and have children and grandchildren. I'm sorry to hear that Dennis died, but knowing you, I'm sure you had many happy years together. And how would it have been with us? I was everywhere after Paris, a rootless itinerant for years before returning to New York and San Francisco and eventually back home, to Los Angeles. Everyone back to the roots. How could a life like that have been better for you than a life surrounded by loving family in Devon? I married again, yes, and now that marriage is on the brink. I've become a curmudgeon. Her friends won't see me. I don't have any of my own. Be happy you were spared such company.

Andy

. . .

How many couples meet for breakfast on their first date? Or actually brunch, if there was such a thing in Paris. It might have been lunch, for both started work at two o'clock, but lunch meant wine and too much food, and neither was in the mood for that before a full day's work. It was spring and the weather was fresh, so they met on the terrace at Fouquet's on the Champs Élysées. He took a table just off the Avenue George V where he could watch for her. She'd said she lived on Avenue Niel, near Ternes, and would be walking. Another walker. That was a good sign.

He spied her crossing the Champs, pausing midway between the pedestrian guards to let the traffic pass. She wore a swishy beige skirt and brown sweater with a blue scarf and smiled and waved when she spotted him. Even more gorgeous by day than by night, he thought. Watching her, he wondered what he was doing. This was the kind of girl he could fall for, and he couldn't afford falling. Or could he? He rarely saw his wife anymore.

"Well, here I am," she said, cheerfully, holding out a hand with silver bracelets, "ready for a big breakfast after a long walk. I haven't eaten a thing since last night."

"No English breakfasts here," he said, "but the omelets are good."

"And croissants."

"Croissants, of course."

A waiter came, they ordered and made idle talk until he was back with the coffee pot and cups. He wondered how a girl like this could be available in a place like Paris. But was she available?

"You like walking?"

"I walk everywhere, sometimes even to work, which is exactly five kilometers from where I live. Most days I take the bus, the 93, which runs to Levallois."

"You don't walk home, I hope."

She laughed. "At night? I'm not that brave."

"What brought you to Paris?"

She smiled. "Ah, *monsieur …*"

He laughed. "I understand."

"What do you understand?"

She'd caught him. "Well, maybe I don't."

"I'm half French. My aunt lives here."

"You live with your aunt?"

Again she laughed. "Oh, no. You don't know my aunt. I live alone."

"A girl like you alone in Paris?"

"I think sometimes I'm the only single girl at the hospital."

"The doctors aren't single?"

"Not a one."

The omelets came, along with a basket of croissants.

"Where were you trained, here or in England?"

"I'm not trained as a nurse. They want to send me to London for a full course. I haven't decided. I'm a bit squeamish, you see."

"I'm squeamish, too."

He wondered what she saw in him. But she'd come, hadn't she? She was remarkably lovely: head of dark curls, luscious red mouth, high *pommettes*, slightly sad smile. He'd have to tell her eventually. And then, would she come again?

"So it's your mother who's French?"

"Yes, Daddy is English. He's a history prof, very conservative, not too keen on having his daughter running around Paris. Doesn't really approve of Paris. Aunt Clotilde found the job at the hospital so he wouldn't worry about me."

"And your mother?"

"She's happy enough in England. Couldn't get Daddy over here if she tried."

"How did they ever meet?"

"In the war. Where else?"

They fell silent. "This is nice," he said, dumbly.

"I never get to places like this," she said.

"My newspaper is right around that corner," he said, pointing toward the rue de Berri. "Sometimes I come here alone. Watch the people. There's no better corner in Paris."

The waiter emptied what was left in the coffee pot into their cups, took the plates and extra croissants and left the check. It was close to aperitif time. Tables were filling up.

"It must be exciting to be a journalist in Paris. So much going on."

"Not quite as exciting as when de Gaulle was running things."

"Ah, de Gaulle. Daddy hated him."

He laughed. The French and the English. The oldest of stories.

"How long have you been here?" she asked.

"I arrived in '67."

"You covered the riots?"

"I did."

"I came just afterward. De Gaulle had just left."

The waiter picked up the fifty franc note and made change. Andy pushed the change back to him.

"Can we do this again?" he asked.

"I'd love to."

"It wouldn't be right if I didn't tell you that I am married."

"Oh, I knew that," she said, standing, holding out her hand. "But thanks for telling me."

"How in the world ...?"

A small smile. "A girl can tell."

. . .

He was down at 6:15 the next morning, an hour earlier than usual. Max started early, and he had no intention of keeping him waiting. He got the coffee brewing while he ate an orange and toasted the bread. Carbs, Max said, and make sure you have a good pee before joining me. At our age, you know. He didn't know Max's age, couldn't really tell with the floppy hat and bandana, but he was up there. Finished, he washed his dish and cup, left the house and set out down toward Montana. A low sun peeked over the mountains to the east. He smelled smoke from up there somewhere.

They met at 24th and Montana, Max dressed in the same jeans, sweater and bandana. It was nippy, cold almost for spring, but would warm up. The kind of day hard to dress for. Max had brought two sacks with straps and two pickers, or grabbers as he called them. "These are the best," he said, handing him one. "Adjustable for any size. Trigger activated. Try it." He hadn't pulled the bandana up, and Andy saw that they were roughly the same age, though on second glance, he wasn't sure. Max had the weathered face of a man who could be seventy or ninety. He wouldn't be doing this at ninety, would he? Suddenly he wondered why he was doing it himself. He hadn't really committed, but here he was. Max had expected him.

"That's Franklin Elementary," said Max, pointing behind him. "Schools are good neighborhoods for trash—even when not in session. You take this side. Signal me when your bag's full, and I'll show you where the trashcans are. You don't have a scarf?"

He put on his mask.

"You up for this?"

"I'll let you know."

They walked for three hours, up and down the many cross streets, filling a bag each. The time went fast, though not fast enough for his knees, which were aching. Santa Monica is laid out like most cities, streets go one way, avenues the other. At ten o'clock, outside Lincoln Middle School on 14th, Max crossed over. "Good work. I know a place on Wilshire where we can get a bagel and coffee. First empty the bags."

It was a café called Murph's with three tables outside and tables and red leather booths inside, an old-fashioned place that looked like it had been there a while but maybe not for much longer. A friendly waitress greeted Max by name, and they settled into a booth and ordered bagels and coffee. Andy took off his mask, Max brought down his bandana. It was a good face: weathered, leathered, solid, a face you could trust.

"Well?"

Andy smiled. "Good exercise."

"You look in good shape."

"So do you."

"Not bad for past eighty."

"And the secret is picking trash."

"You might say so."

"Why?"

"You're persistent with your whys, aren't you?"

The waitress was back with their bagels and filled the coffee cups. "First time I've seen you with company, Max."

"Good man, Agnes. Kept up with me."

"They seem to know you here," said Andy when she was gone.

"Come by Murph's most days. Stash my bike here."

"You live close?"

"Venice."

"Why don't you do Venice neighborhoods?'

"Do those, too," he said, biting into a bagel.

"Why, Max?"

"Why, why, you are relentless."

He wasn't bald, but didn't have much hair either. Face showed experience more than age, its salient feature the strange brown eyes behind the spectacles. Owl-like, his eyes turned with his head. Calm, slow-moving, a man of composure. Finally, he smiled. "Do you know how often Santa Monica cleans its streets?"

"I do know," Andy said, "I live here."

"Once a month. That means, on average, thirty days a month for trash and one for trash removal. That seem right to you?"

"This isn't Hell's Kitchen," you know."

"Ah, you know Hell's Kitchen."

"I worked in New York."

"So did I. Came west for my health."

"Smoke from these fires can't be good for your health."

"Didn't have fires when I came. As far west as I'm going to go."

He started to take out his wallet, but Andy beat him to it, extracting a ten and handing it with the check to Agnes. "Keep the change."

Max watched. "You're generous," he said.

"These are hard times for small businesses."

"Yes," said Max, standing. "You never told me your name."

"I'm Andy."

"You going to join me again, Andy?" he asked as they walked out.

"You going to tell me why you do it?"

He stopped, looked Andy up and down, once around the restaurant, waving to Agnes, and back to Andy. Slow, steady. "Not to clean the streets, if that's what you mean."

"Why then?"

"Just do it."

"Just do it?"

"Just do it."

Home by eleven, Nancy was gone, likely to the club. She'd brought in the newspaper he'd forgotten in his hurry not to be late for Max. He couldn't remember the last time he'd forgotten to bring in the newspaper. Murph's bagel had not been enough, so he made an omelet and poured the coffee she'd left in the press. Too strong, he poured milk in the cup and warmed it in the microwave. He sat down to read about an armada of oil tankers spread out for miles along the California coast. The story jumped inside to a photo of another armada in the North Sea stretching halfway down the coast of Denmark. The tankers couldn't land because nobody wanted their oil. Economies shutting down around the world as the plague raged and oceans turned into a giant tanker parking lot, waiting for one of them to spring a leak. A frontpage story with color photos showed forest fires up and down California. A guy in the Santa Cruz Mountains got lost on the roads, trapped by the fires, incinerated in his truck.

Needing a rest after the mornings exertions, he went into his den, took off his shoes and unfolded the cotton blanket he kept on the daybed. Remembering that he hadn't checked the computer that morning, he turned it on. He had only one message.

Dear Andy,

Thank you for being so honest about your life, but you forget one thing. I was in love with you. I should have been there to endure the pain with you, to share it with you. I would have done anything for you, gone anywhere. That's what love is.

Having read your books now, I know that we have different views of love. You're a writer, a skeptic. In those days, I was just a silly girl. But I remember exactly how I felt about you. I hurt physically when I couldn't see you, hold you. Oh, I understood the difference between us, how many more demands were upon you than I would ever have. What demands could a lowly nurse trainee living in a tiny flat on Avenue Niel have upon her? I was so happy when you called and we could set something up. Too many nights I got off the bus and walked home wondering what my life was coming to and why I was still in Paris. The answer was because of you. I knew you couldn't call or drop by all the time, but in those days it was hard for me to distinguish be-

tween couldn't and wouldn't. All I knew was that I didn't have you when I wanted you, and that made me very unhappy.

If I'd known what was happening to you I would have stayed. That's what's so cruel. And had you known you would have told me, n'est-ce pas? You didn't write much from New York, three letters is all I remember before leaving the hospital, but you never mentioned your wife. You rarely mentioned her to me, though it was clear that you were unhappy. I dwell on these things now, though I know I shouldn't. Had I known, what would I have done? It was better the way things turned out, you say, but when your heart is broken it's hard to see the sunny side.

Philippa

His mind spinning, he turned off the computer, pulled down the dark shades and laid down under the blanket. He seemed to be escaping into some new world. And why not? Philippa Grey was carrying him back a half century, making the old world new again. It didn't matter how much time had passed, she would always be the twenty-something girl crossing the Champs Élysées, waving to him in her swishy skirt. Thinking on her carried his mind back to hundreds of exciting days and nights buried too long under the blanket of time and routine. I would have done anything for you, she wrote, gone anywhere. Why had he let her go? They'd had something and mindlessly let it slip away. *He'd* let it slip away. Now they were trying to find it again, if only in their memories. We reinvent the world each time we remember something. And why not? It was a far better place back then.

But was it? The world he'd covered as a correspondent was the world of the Cold War, the Berlin Wall, the Cultural Revolution, spies, nuclear bombs, wars, riots and revolutions. Why did it seem so much better than the world of today? Or was it just that we were young lovers in Paris, blind to everything? The shades made his room pitch dark, but he closed his eyes anyway. He'd laid down to sleep, but found his mind spinning.

Let it spin, he had to settle this thing burning in him: Why were things so dreadful today, dreadful to the point that he'd lost all hope, something that never happened before, even in the Cold War days, even as his life fell apart in Paris, losing his wife, his girlfriend, his self-confidence, and nearly his job in the space of a month. But he'd recovered, gotten on with his life, even had some success. What chance for recovery existed for a world today in the hands of sociopathic egotists pushing civilization to the point of no return and being cheered on by howling sycophants. Against evil we can fight; against stupidity we are helpless.

They said that Trump could lose the election but not leave, would challenge the result and not concede; if forced out he would start plotting a return through a Republican Party whose corruption already had infected the courts and state legislatures. Meanwhile, Andy McKnight, the eccentric, the pariah, the crank, would go on losing friends and yet another wife, escaping into the past and into a strange friendship with Max, a man who cleaned streets, seeking to do something, anything, to save what was left of his sanity.

There'd been a logic to events in the old days, an equilibrium that kept the world going despite the crazy things that humans did. Was it because we knew we were posturing, that two world wars were enough for everyone,

and no one had the stomach for a third, especially with nuclear bombs? Or because our quarrels had a greater sense
of theater than of reality, knowing we could call the play
off anytime we wanted—as we did. Was the difference that
people then still basically trusted each other, believed that
reason would prevail and that institutions had permanently replaced the power-hungry megalomaniacs of the past?
Germany was soon to be a reunited democracy; Russia and
China were run by collectivist politburos, not aggressive,
ruthless dictators. We clung to our systems, yes, but strove to
settle differences short of war. Terrible mistakes were made,
but things settled down. The danger was too great.

Today, a nihilist comes to the White House at the very
moment the planet is beginning its death rattle. A plague
arrives. Nature and humanity gradually waste away, but
the nihilist ignores, denies, defiles. The air warms, the seas
rise, the glaciers melt, the forests burn, the storms rage, the
virus surges. He preens; he lies. Democratic Europe is our
enemy; Russia, back in the hands of a ruthless dictator, is
our friend, as is North Korea, less a country than a military
concentration camp. America is great, the nihilist bellows,
cheered on by mobs and his media toadies. The 250-year-
old Constitution that facilitated the election of a man who
lost the election by three million votes is further subverted
as he takes control of the two other branches of government,
putative counterweights to the executive. Congress curtsies.
The courts are stacked. Alliances are eroded, pacts annulled,
commerce disrupted, internal opposition crushed under an
onslaught of lies and distortions.

He awoke in a sweat. Had he cried out in his sleep? But
was he asleep? He listened. Not a sound.

Chapter 5

The refrigerator was almost empty. Odd he hadn't noticed earlier. Eggs, but no fruit or bread. No milk. Nancy hadn't been to the store, so he would have to go himself. She might stop at the store on the way back from the club, but she might not. Sometimes they both went and bought too much; sometimes they thought the other was going and bought nothing. They didn't leave notes anymore. The clock said one-thirty. He'd slept over an hour recovering from his morning ordeal. He wondered about Max. "I'm here most days at ten o'clock," he said as they left Murph's. He gave him the picker. "Incentive to come back."

In the car, he headed down San Vicente to Seventh Street, turning onto Entrada, past the Santa Monica Stairs, past Rustic Canyon, on to the beach. He hadn't been in the ocean since returning from the islands. The parking lot was only partly filled, as was the beach, strange site at Will Rogers, ordinarily busy on a fine spring day. People were social distancing in small groups, some with masks, some without. He placed his wallet in the glove compartment, pulled off his sweatshirt, grabbed his neoprene top and a towel, locked the car, zipped a single key into his swimming shorts and headed for the ocean. It felt good to be back on the beach, his beach. He could have checked the water temps before coming, but had not. Somewhere in the mid-sixties, he imagined. To the north he spied a few surfers, but no swimmers. He dropped his towel, pulled on his top, put the eighty-degree water of Hanalei out of his mind and plunged in, heading straight out. Cold-water swimmers, he'd read, developed a protein that restored brain tissue and memory and protected against dementia. He couldn't remember the name of the protein. Needed more cold water.

Home at five with two bags of groceries, Nancy's car already in the garage. From the cracking of the water heater, she was in her bath. He went into the kitchen and loaded the fridge, which still was empty. If he ended up with another omelet, at least it would be with ham and cheese. And a salad. She hadn't been shopping which meant she wouldn't be around for dinner. He put off a shower, cracked a beer, avoided the front page of the newspaper and turned to the weather page to check how close he was on the water temps. Sixty-six, about right for early spring. The protein was called RBM3 he suddenly remembered, no doubt thanks to the cold swim. He took his beer and the newspaper and headed into the living room.

"Hello Andy."

She was dressed for going out in designer jeans and a beige silk blouse. Pearl pendant he'd given her at the neck and rings and dangles. Her dark hair, which she gave a little help, was up. She looked good. Age did not have to mean decline, on the contrary. She stood by the entrance to the room, distant.

"I hope you bought some food," she said.

"I stopped on Montana. You off somewhere?"

"Bridge night."

"Ah ... at?"

"Chuck's house."

"Chuck Collins?"

"Remember him?"

"Of course. His wife died, didn't she?"

"A few years ago. We went to the funeral."

"Ah yes, right."

Even across the room he could see that something was bothering her. It had to be more than his comments at the Godfreys.

"We don't see much of each other anymore," he said.

She cinched the bag up on her shoulder. "No, we don't."

He stood and crossed toward her. "You want to tell me something?"

She held her ground. "I thought it was you who would tell me something."

"What would I be telling you?"

"Shouldn't there be something?"

He was puzzled. Nancy was not mysterious.

"No, I don't think so."

She turned to go. "Good-bye, Andy."

"Say hello to Chuck for me."

She wouldn't.

They'd never had conversations like that in the past, short staccato exchanges with words used to cover up thoughts rather than express them. They used to be good at conversation, not anything profound, Nancy wasn't a big reader but stayed informed and able to keep a good palaver going. She was a cheerful person, content with her life and the decisions she'd made, above all, to leave the farm and come west. She'd never shown any past sign of regret over giving up her independence to become Mrs. McKnight. She had her moods, but knew how to pull out of them. She was an admirable woman, generous and courageous, popular with women because she was friendly and loyal and with men because she was friendly and attractive. She knew how to defend herself, would not be bullied.

He knew she didn't like the changes in her husband, but what could he do about it? There was a peril out there, and if others did not see it, it was his job to alert them. He saw her frustration, but it did not compare with his own.

Paris isn't good to everyone, and he knew the stories. It wasn't always good to him, especially at the beginning. The marriage was a mistake, but both wanted to try. His work, too, had ups and downs. He'd landed in Paris as just one more American drifter, a guy from California who'd worked on a few newspapers and been fired in almost as many places as he'd worked. Turned out the *Herald Tribune* needed a copy editor, and he'd come at the right time. Problem was that he'd never been a copy editor, always a reporter, always a writer. He might not have lasted except that the newspaper got a new owner and a new editor fresh from New York named Arthur Schwartz. He met Artie about the same time he met Philippa.

Together, they changed his life around. For reasons he never fully understood, the new editor liked him, took to inviting him across the street to the bar at the Hotel California, something he didn't do with everybody. They had almost nothing in common. Artie was twice his age, a bald Jew from the Bronx who'd worked his way up to city editor on the *New York Herald Tribune* and never been west of the Mississippi. Neither of them spoke much French in the beginning, and neither fit in with the crowd of jaded, multi-lingual professional expatriates who'd been at the *Herald Tribune* forever and knew Paris as well as any cabdriver. One thing they did have in common was marriages that weren't working.

Artie saw that his talents were wasted as copy editor, made him a reporter again and, with time, he became the newspaper's chief European correspondent. Without Artie, everything would have been different. He'd have lost his job, lost his marriage sooner rather than later, lost Paris and gone back to drifting. He would not have met Philippa Grey. There's someone like Artie in everybody's life, or should be—the mentor, the roshi, the guardian angel—the person who sees something in you you didn't know was there and helps you dig it out.

There was a steak-frites place on the rue du Débarcadère, up the street from his apartment on the Place St.-Ferdinand. It wasn't a steak-frites place in the neighborhood bistro sense where you eat fatty steak and greasy frites at a Formica table for eight francs, but in the nouvelle cuisine sense where the steak is lean, the frites are delicate and the only thing that's fat is the check. There's always a line to get in. He'd sometimes taken his wife there before she decamped to the country. Chez Henri had no stars and was in the 17th Arrondissement, not the smartest part of town, but Andy thought it would be a fine place for his second date with Philippa. When he reached her by phone at the hospital, she said she'd never been there.

"It's only ten minutes from where you live—on foot."

"I'm sure I couldn't afford it."

"I would have assumed you weren't paying."

She laughed. "I hope I'm not."

"So where do you go when you go out to dinner?"

"I don't go out to dinner very much."

"Hospital hours?"

"If you like."

It was another Wednesday. He offered to pick her up, but she said she would walk over. You never know about Paris weather in April, and that April was typical, some days summer by day and winter by night, some days the opposite or neither. It was misting as he waited in line for her, but wasn't raining. Not yet. He'd told her eight-thirty and showed up early to get in line. Henri did not take reservations. He watched for her coming up rue St.-Ferdinand.

She wore a Burberry's beige trench, cinched tightly, with matching scarf, and she carried an umbrella. All very English. Heads turned as she stepped into line with him. As on their first date, he found himself wondering about her. A girl this alluring deserved better than hospital bedpans, wet nights with umbrellas and dates with a married man. She belonged in *le tout Paris*—aperitifs in St.-Germain, evenings at the Comédie française, souper at les Halles and midnight in Montmartre. The French admire beauty and style above all things, and there is no way that a girl like Philippa Grey could escape their notice for long.

They ordered the Henri's usual—steak-frites, salad and Beaujolais. There were about twenty tables, and they were crammed with the low-level, contented sounds Parisians make in front of a good, simple French meal. No worries about too many calories from foie gras, oeufs en hollandaise and boeuf bourguignon. Such fare was for Michelin. Henri was steaks, frites and a single desert, tarte Tatin. Henri had no pretensions.

"So how are things at the hospital?" he said after they'd ordered. "I don't know much about hospitals. Fortunately."

"Hospitals are not happy places, though we do try. The work completely exhausts you, tolerable only if you regard medicine as a mission."

"And you do?"

She thought it over. "I think I might like to. It hasn't happened."

"Is it something you can learn—to love a hospital?"

"Hmm, maybe the American Hospital, much more elegant than our little place. Surely you've been there."

"My doctor is at the American Hospital. You've been there, I take it. For work?"

She hesitated. "No, a doctor I know."

He felt a chill. What doctor? Tom Heinrich—his doctor? No, Tom was married. But then, so was he.

"Do you use French doctors?" she asked, not offering more. "They're free, you know."

The wine came in a carafe, along with a tray of baguette slices. He poured. His mind returned.

"I did once. Only once. My wife Claire's doctor, Dr. Ben-Said. I had an abdominal pain, sharp, like appendicitis. Dr. BS, as I came to call him, referred me to the local clinic overnight for tests and treatment. He had the charts when he came in the next day and said they showed nothing unusual. I said the pain is still there, doctor, not as bad, but still there."

Chez Henri moved quickly, white-aproned waiters with full trays in constant motion. It never took long to get served. Outside, the line had not lessened but you were never hurried at Henri's. People in line knew the system, knew that eventually they would be seated and wouldn't want to be hurried either. Henri was gaining a reputation. He had mastered the French fry.

Their order arrived, and he watched her eat, hungrily but delicately in the European way, fork always in the left hand.

"So what happened?"

"He asked me how I felt about Vietnam."

"*Comment?*"

"Exactly what I said. He offered that the Vietnam War might be causing my abdominal problems. Psychological reaction, that sort of thing."

"What did you say?"

He took a sip of Beaujolais and poured more for both of them. "It took willpower not to say something rude. I knew the French were conflicted over Vietnam—hated the idea that Americans might succeed where they'd failed, but hated just as much that the Vietnamese would win again. I told him I didn't really think much about Vietnam, which was the truth."

"So what caused your problem?"

"Turned out to be a hiatal hernia, diagnosed and treated at the American Hospital."

She laughed. "I may have to share that story with my colleagues."

They'd both walked to the restaurant. He lived just down the street. Her street, Avenue Niel, was a little farther on, off the Avenue des Ternes. It was misting a little heavier when they finished dinner, but still not raining. He planned to walk her home. He liked the Avenue des Ternes, wide, friendly shopping street with not too much traffic at night. He liked the 17th Arrondissement, bourgeois in the French sense rather than chic like the 7th, 8th, or 16th or proletariat like much of the rest. When they reached the avenue, she stopped and turned, holding out her hand.

"You don't have to walk me home, Andy. I know my way like an old dog."

Philippa Grey was the last person he would ever compare to an old dog, but he hesitated. He wanted to keep going, wanted to walk with her, to be invited up to her flat, wanted anything that might follow. He felt that she might want the same thing, but he was being asked to leave. He did not want to leave. He did not want to go home alone.

"I'd like to walk you home."

"I know. Maybe next time."

She kissed him on the cheek. "Good-night, Andy."

He watched her go, putting up the umbrella against the mist. He felt desolate. He couldn't help it, wondering about the doctor at the American Hospital.

Chapter 6

Dear Philippa,

Your letter moved me to tears. It's the first time anyone ever said things like that to me. On this planet being destroyed by man's war on nature and nature's revenge, my solace, my one escape, is your letters and the memories you bring flooding back. I'm afraid to open my computer lest I don't find something from you. Are you to save me once again? You did once before, but you already know that. How many times did I tell you? When we met that night at Churchill's, I was lost. I'd been happy at first—happy to be in Paris, happy to be with a great newspaper, happy to be married. And in the space of a year, I was a failure at everything, ready to pack up.

It took us time, didn't it? You were cautious, and I couldn't believe that a girl like you could be interested in me, someone so wrapped up in his own miseries, his own selfishness. On our second date you told me about seeing the doctor at the American Hospital, and after that I couldn't get through to you and didn't know your address and thought it was over before it began. Then something happened. You never told me what it was. Maybe the tenth time I phoned the hospital they didn't hang up but got you on the line and you invited me to Avenue

Niel for dinner—the dinner interrupted by Claire and her Normandy farmhouse. But I won't go into that. We both know the story too well.

You and Artie arrived in my life at the same time, and I stopped thinking about throwing myself in the Seine—which wouldn't have worked anyway because I like cold water. From that moment on— until I left for New York—it was bliss. I remember you saying you hated your place on the Avenue Niel, but I loved it. I remember everything about that flat: the creaky old stairs, the bedroom so small that we had to get out at the foot of the bed, the funny little minifridge, the stovetop you made do in place of an oven in the area you called a kitchen, the shower you could not turn around in. Amazing what the French can do when they have no space. I loved every part of it and fell madly in love with you.

Why did I accept the assignment in New York? You never said a thing, but I knew how you felt about it. Even Artie advised against it, but I thought it was the right career move, and no one could tell Andy McKnight what to do in those days. I assumed everything would resume as before when I returned to Paris. Everything would wait for me. But you were gone, and I understood why you were gone. I had treated you foolishly, miserably, selfishly. I had taken you for granted. I got what I deserved and have regretted it ever since.

What if ...? What if ...? There are so many what ifs in everybody's life, but that is the one that haunts me.

Andy

The parked cars with plates from across Normandy stretched up both sides of the single lane leading to the farmhouse. The previous times he'd visited Claire's farm he'd been able to drive through the main gate into the central grass courtyard. This time the gate was closed. He turned the car around, drove back to where the line began and parked. Walking back down the lane, he heard loud voices and loud music, a din really, rising up from the walls and engulfing the quiet countryside. He wished he'd brought a bottle of Canadian Club. Everybody would be drinking pastis, which he hated. In the beginning he'd meant to leave a bottle of Canadian at the farm, but in the beginning he didn't know he wouldn't like the farm, that Claire wouldn't mind that he didn't like it, and that he wouldn't mind that she didn't mind. The door through the stone wall to the courtyard was open, and he entered a scene that might have been done by Breughel: "Summer Revelry on the Farm."

She'd insisted that he come, something she'd never done before. It was to be a grand housewarming, a *pendaison de crémaillère* to celebrate the end of construction on the main building, and her husband should be there. People didn't need to know they weren't together in Paris anymore.

He couldn't very well have told her he couldn't come because he was seeing another woman, so there he was. The party was to start at four, and he was a little late, but this noisy affair had clearly been going for some time. A French rock group was jamming on the grass, complete with amplifiers. The low buildings at the rear and along one side of the courtyard for animals and storage were still in construction, being transformed into cottages. The main building, a long, two-story structure where the Chabret family, Claire's maternal side, had lived for a few centuries, had been rebuilt, refurnished and was ready for occupancy. Claire had a family loan to cover costs. From the exterior, it looked like a good job, drab stone farmhouse transformed into elegant country manor. The outlying buildings would be finished and soon ready for the army of Chabret cousins who would descend for weekends. Or weeks. Or longer.

"*An-dee, An-dee*, enfin!"

They spoke mostly French now, though her English was as good as his French and their conversations came out in a personalized version of Franglais. From deep in the crush, she'd seen him arrive and was cutting a swath across the grass like a navy cruiser, spreading a wave of cousins in her wake. He recognized some of the crowd from their wedding, where he'd met most of them for the first and only time.

They kissed on both cheeks in the accepted manner. "You are late," she said with feigned crossness. She was smiling. Why not? It was a lovely spring day, the sun still high and no sign of rainclouds. She wore a colorful print, low-cut cotton frock, and he could tell there was nothing under it. Her sandy hair was up and she wore no make-up. She looked very French, unchanged from the girl he'd married two years before, the center of attraction, as always. Why she looked French and Philippa English despite the cross-Channel Norman blood in both of them, he couldn't have said. Claire was unchanged, but they both knew that everything had changed. Their marriage was a charade likely to go on only until she found a suitable reason for announcing its end.

"It is all of four-thirty," he said.

"We got started a little early," said Hubert, one cousin he did remember. A contractor from Dreux, Hubert held a glass of the strong, green, milky stuff they drank.

"No cadeau?" asked Hubert.

He'd completely forgotten that you're supposed to bring something for the housewarming. "But I am the husband," he said, laughing. "I am excused."

"Yes," said Claire happily. "You are excused." She waved her arm around the terrain. "So, what do you think?"

"I think you've done a grand job," he said. "Bravo."

"He does not get out here too often," she said. "Andy does not like the country."

"Dommage," said Hubert, unconvincingly. He was in charge of construction. Claire once told him that Hubert, un ami d'enfance, had always been in love with her.

"But he is your cousin," Andy protested.

"Distant cousin," she said. Then: "Fairly distant."

"Ah, vous Americains" he said. "Ne pas aimer la campagne n'est pas francais."

"Unfortunately," Andy replied in very correct French, "no newspapers are published in la campagne. I have to work in the city."

"Yes, yes," said Claire, uncomfortable with the exchange. "But I am so glad you could come. I was afraid you'd be off on some story. You're not too lonely in Paris?"

"I am desperate, of course, but what can I do? I have my job."

"Of course, of course," she said, laughing. "Now come on and mix with my friends. They all want to see you."

He doubted that.

As luck would have it, that was the Sunday Philippa had finally invited him over for dinner. He could have lied to Claire, could have told her he would be gone on assignment. He badly wanted to see Philippa and had thought about a little social lie. But they'd never lied to each other. That's not to say they told each other everything. He'd never asked about

Hubert because she would have told him. She'd never asked what he did in Paris while she was gone because he would have told her. But the whole family would be present at Anet for the *pendaison* at the farmhouse, and it was no time to embarrass her.

He could have lied to Philippa as well, told her he was suddenly being sent away and couldn't come. He'd worried for too long that he would never see her again. But she'd have known. A girl can tell, she'd said at Fouquet's. But tell what— that you're lying or that you're married? It wouldn't do to try to explain things on the telephone. He needed to see her in person. He called the hospital and asked if she knew the Café La Lorraine on the Place des Ternes, around the corner from where she lived on Avenue Niel. He sometimes stopped there when he was walking to the newspaper, and her bus stop, the 93, was just across the street. They could meet for coffee and then be on their separate ways.

La Lorraine was more restaurant than café, a place specializing in heavy Lorraine cuisine from out there on the German border, things like quiche, sausage, spaetzle, choucroûte, food with lots of pork and lots of cheese. In the warmer months they set up wicker chairs on the sidewalk terrace for people less in need of food than libations. Ternes was only five minutes from his flat on Place St.-Ferdinand, and mornings he sometimes went there alone to buy a newspaper and sit with coffee and croissant in the sunshine. He found a table and looked up to see her crossing Avenue Wagram. He'd expected nurse's white, but she wore jeans and a tight red-and-black checkered blouse, red scarf at the neck. He stood and waved.

"I was looking for nurses' white," he said as she came up.

"Oh no. I always change at work." She offered her hand, not her cheek.

"Red scarf ... means communist, not anarchist, which is black. Code of '68."

She laughed. "I have black scarfs as well."

"White means surrender," he said.

"Too early for that."

They laughed. She looked lovely— young and chic and surely unavailable. Dark eyes, dark hair, scarlet mouth. He wondered about the doctor. American? At the American Hospital it would make sense, but the American Hospital was a multi-national place. They ordered coffee and remembering the reason he invited her felt that sinking feeling. Would there always be something he was afraid to tell her?

She lit a cigarette. First time he'd noticed, though she might have been smoking at Churchill's, he wasn't sure. He hadn't had a cigarette since the army. Interfered too much with his breathing, his swimming.

"First of the day," she said, watching him. "Maybe the last. I don't really like them."

"So?"

"Nerves, I guess. Helps before I get there. I'm in recovery this week. Lots of bad cases." The coffee came. "So how have you been, Andy?"

"Bad couple of weeks. Couldn't get through to a certain girl. Thought maybe she was out of town."

"I'm sorry. I had to sort things out."

"And?"

"They're sorted."

"The doc?"

"The doc."

He wasn't sure which way to take it, didn't ask. They fell silent, watching people pass along the sidewalk, looking across the street to the Ternes Square with its chestnut trees.

April in Paris, chestnuts in blossom. He sipped his coffee, uncomfortable, nervous.

She picked it up. "Something wrong?"

"No. Really happy to see you again."

She stared at him quizzically, but didn't answer.

Silence resumed.

"Why two married men?" she said after a while, surely to herself. She was frowning, debating something. It was hardly the moment to tell her he was breaking their date. "I'm sorry I wouldn't take your calls, Andy. I couldn't."

It was painful. She didn't know how to get at it anymore than he did. She inhaled deeply, keeping the smoke down too long.

"These last two weeks were awful. I didn't know what to do, but more than that, I didn't know who I was anymore. Who am I? What am I? What am I doing in Paris? When am I coming home? It's the question my father asks in every letter. Am I in love? Am I a nurse? Am I French? Am I English? Am I both? Am I neither? For days I've been utterly useless to everybody. The head nurse called me in. I know what she was thinking. It's what they're always thinking. Just like my mother. Am I pregnant? Just what do they think I am?"

Every word resonated. He felt the girl's pain. In a different context it was his own pain. How was he to tell her what he'd brought her here to tell her? Would she understand or would it drive her back to the doc he hoped she was telling him that she'd broken with?

Suddenly, a smile broke through. "Sorry, I didn't mean all that. It just came out. Blurting, Daddy calls it." She put out the cigarette. "Last one. Do you smoke? All the French do, you know." She reached out and touched his hand.

"Yes, I know."

"Well, as I said, things are sorted out and I do have a surprise. Do you know the farmer's market in Levallois? Rue Brossolette, just up from the hospital. I sometimes walk there on market days. Best produce in Paris. On Sunday, you're going to have a farm fresh French meal. You bring the wine, preferably red."

It was time. "Something's come up."

As dark, embarrassed clouds crept cross her face, he tried to explain. He and his wife lived apart. They were still friends, a couple that married too young and had seen their lives and interests grow apart. There were no children. She'd built a house in Normandy and wanted to live there. He worked in Paris and could not leave the city.

The waiter collected the cups, put down the little tray with the bill and left.

He rarely saw Claire, he said, who was, he believed, involved with another man. However, she was having a party Sunday to celebrate the end of construction at her farmhouse, and all the family was to be there. Since they were still married, she'd asked him to be there for the celebration. For some people, appearances matter. He did not want to embarrass her.

He stopped and waited.

"So you can't come over?"

"It would be late."

"You're separated from your wife but you have to be with her."

"This once. Yes. I should be."

"I see."

The waiter returned to pick up the twenty franc note and make change. He did not linger. He understood—if not the language, the sad tones.

She fell silent as he waited for the blade to fall. Her gaze wandered out across the street and the square with the chestnut trees and finally back to him.

"I like you, Andy," she said at length. "I know I shouldn't, but I liked you that first night when you came to our table and listened quietly while Titty and the others went on with their horrible blather about the British Hospital. I don't think you said a word, just nodded and smiled. You smiled at me, do you remember?"

"You were beside me. You and Simon. You were why I came to the table. The hospital was a pretext."

"Yes, and I knew you were married, and I didn't care."

"How did you know?"

"Single men act differently around me."

He wanted to ask about that, but she was not done. "You were honest about it, and you still are. I have to respect that."

The blade had not fallen. Not yet.

Suddenly she was on her feet: "There's my bus."

He stood. "Do I get a raincheck for dinner?"

She held out her hand. "I don't know. I really don't. I've quite lost my bearings. What *am* I doing in Paris?"

She ran for her bus.

Chapter 7

Whenever he ran into Nancy, which wasn't often because she was avoiding him, she had nothing to say. He wanted to talk, but she'd started waiting until he had finished breakfast to come down and most nights stayed out late for dinner and bridge. All this was totally unlike her, and he didn't know what to make of it. It had to be more than his comments at the Godfreys, which were nothing she hadn't heard before. Wasn't there something he wanted to tell her, she'd asked on her way out the other night. If saying something would have cleared the air he'd gladly have said it, but he had no idea what she meant.

One evening he came home from the ocean and was surprised to find her in the kitchen. He saw pasta, smelled garlic. Good signs.

"Pesto," she said, in a cheery voice that was the old Nancy. "Fresh basil I found at the farmers' market on Pico. And a baguette, of course."

"I've got just the pinot noir for it," he said before heading upstairs.

While showering he thought back. What did she want from him? What was she expecting him to say? Ask for a separation? He would never do that. Even in normal times he wouldn't do that, but in the time of the two plagues it was the last thing on his mind. He loved this woman. But did *she* want a separation? Did she think life might be better with some clubby bon vivant who wouldn't ruin her social life? Walk out after thirty-five years? Try a fling with pudgy, boring, bridge-playing Chuck Collins? Preposterous. They'd always been happy together. Always. Still, the thought passed his mind that maybe that's why she was cooking dinner: a good pasta and wine to make the execution easier.

He dressed quickly, brushed his hair and was downstairs to open the wine and pour two glasses. He handed her one and kissed her cheek. He hadn't done that for a while. She grabbed his hand for a moment, then dropped it and turned back to the stove.

Dinner was mostly chitchat. He told her about RBM3 and earned a smile. He tried to read her mood, tried to understand what this was all about. They hadn't had a normal night at home since returning from Hawaii, so there had to be an explanation. It seemed at times that she was about to open up, but then she backed off, wouldn't get into it.

The bottle was mostly empty by the end of dinner, and they'd shared it equally, unusual for her, not much of a drinker. Something was coming.

She started to get up to clear the table, but sat back down, fixing him with a hard eye and saying in a flat voice: "I want to understand you, Andy. I have to understand you."

He nodded. "You know what it is, honey," he said, as slowly and apologetically as he could. "I'm desperately worried about what is happening."

Her eyes widened. "To us?"

"Yes, of course. But not just to us. To everyone. There is no us anymore."

She flushed. "*No us* … that's terrible. How can you say that?"

He felt a stab of annoyance. He hadn't meant it that way at all.

"Why can't you understand that it's something bigger than just us. The good news is that the destruction of the human race might be good for the planet, give it time to purge the human poison out of the system before regenerating."

A down-to-earth, practical, sensible woman with neither a speculative nor especially inquisitive mind, she stared down at her hands, letting what he just said sink in before replying. "I said I want to understand you, Andy. I should say, I want to understand you again. For thirty-five years I have understood you. We have understood each other. We've been friends, lovers, partners. Now we're lost. You say things, to me and to others ..."

He waited for her to finish the sentence, but she did not.

"Imagine," he said, "that everyone suddenly decided to act together; to do everything in their power to save the planet from coal and oil and plastic and carbon dioxide and let the fires recede and the seas settle and land heal and waters cleanse and animal life return and glaciers reform and coral reefs grow. If we all acted together, do you think we could do these things?"

She just stared. "You're hopeless, you know."

"Really. Do you think we could do it?"

She shook her head. "Be realistic for once."

"Sometimes I think I'm the only one who is realistic. In a thousand years, a better race of beings will exist and ask: How could they have been so stupid? They destroyed themselves."

"Oh, Andy, *stop!* Forget the planet for a minute. What is happening to us?"

"*We* are responsible," he said, too loudly. "Why can't you understand that? We all have to act together. Start by electing someone who spells it out like FDR did in the war: these are the things we have to do; these are the things we have to give up; this is the price we have to pay. All of us. Together."

Slowly, mutely, she shook her head.

"We elected FDR four times," he said.

"I can't reach you anymore. We are in different orbits."

She rose to start clearing, start rinsing, her back to him, looking outside to the shadows from the lights beyond the pines. Suddenly, she turned off the water and spun to face him. "We can't go on like this, you know."

"What did you mean the other day when you asked if there was something I wanted to tell you?"

She stared. *"Well?"*

"I don't get it."

And she stood there, staring, water dripping, anxiety stamped on her handsome face. "We have to talk about it. We've never had secrets."

"What secret?"

She turned back around. Maddening. Whatever it was, it was up to him.

Instead of swimming the next day, he set out after breakfast on a walk. The pesto hadn't worked. Nancy was waiting for him to leave to come downstairs. The mood in the house was approaching unbearable. Standing outside, letting sunshine filter through a tall pine to brighten his mood, he closed his eyes, waiting for inspiration to tell him which direction to take.

"Mr. McKnight, are you all right?"

Surprised, he opened his eyes to see Elly Lancaster, the teenage daughter of neighborhood friends, staring at him. She pulled her green scarf down. "Sorry, I didn't mean to startle you."

His mask was in his pocket, but she stood off at a distance. "Not at all. I was meditating on which path to take."

She smiled. "Physically or spiritually?"

"Ha, that's good. Let's say both."

She was a pretty girl, maybe not even a teenager any-more. So easy to lose track of those who are a half-century younger. She was at UCLA, he remembered, one of the lucky locals to be admitted to a school whose chances for admission were proportional to the distance they lived away from Los Angeles. Her parents, Sam and Patricia Lancaster, lived on 24th, though he hadn't seen them in ages. They'd been closer in his club days, though Sam's doctrinaire rigidity had always been a pain. Patricia was in one of Nancy's bridge groups. He'd known Elly all her life. They'd gone to her christening.

"We all need something, don't we?" she said.

The comment caught his attention. Sam Lancaster was a UCLA economics professor and a libertarian, but Elly's com-ment didn't sound very libertarian.

"Are you walking?" he asked.

"Actually, I'm running, but I'll gladly walk with you a bit if you don't mind."

"You can bring me up to date on the news. We were in Kauai."

He looked closer as they turned toward San Vicente. Attractive, with short dark hair, she looked the athlete she'd always been, feminine and graceful. She was a good club ten-nis player, and he tried to remember something else she did, something unusual. He searched his mind. For a moment it wouldn't come, but as they walked along it popped in. Fencing, Elly was a fencer. Odd sport for Southern California. She wore an outfit with runners' shoes, tights and various T-shirts.

"School shut down, I hear."

"They say your junior year's the most important, and I'm spending mine alone in front of a computer at home. No

classes, no sports, no friends, no life. I'm getting the feeling
next year will be the same." She shot a glance at him as they
walked. "Depends."

"Depends?"

She was studying him. "You know what I mean."

He had a hunch, but she would have to spill it. "Some of
us old guys forget how much harder it is for young people.
How are your folks taking things?"

"We don't talk anymore."

"Ah."

Didn't go to class, didn't talk to her parents, was giving
up running to tag along with him, this was a girl who needed
to open up. She was cautious, sounding him out, probably
wondering if he was a libertarian like her father. He glanced
over at her as they came to Carlyle. More of Sam in her than
Patricia. Sam's cheekbones. Honest face. Something stub-
born in it. He'd gotten along with Sam in the day. Stayed off
economics with him. Decent tennis player.

They stood on the curb, letting a car pass. "I'm losing
boyfriends, girlfriends, old friends, slowly losing my mind.
We're in the middle of this ... this ... catastrophe, and the
man in the White House does everything to make it worse."

"Do you talk about it with your parents?"

She looked both ways on Carlyle, considering traffic,
considering how to answer the question. "No," she said, at
length. "We don't talk. I'd move out if I had someplace to go.
They think I've turned into some kind of radical and want me
to quit UCLA and enroll in a right-wing rich kids religious
school like Pepperdine."

He thought about it as they crossed and turned toward
the country club. If it was like this in Santa Monica, how
much worse it must be in places like Texas or Iowa or Indiana

where the people listened to Fox News all day and believed every lie that was passed on from the White House. How much worse it was at her age. College was meant to be as much the joy of student society as the value of the classroom, and she was deprived of both. The worst that could happen to him was to be thrown out of some ex-friend's house where he didn't want to be anyway and losing communication with his wife. This girl was losing her youth.

They walked a while in the shade of the tall pines. "I know you have running to do, Elly. How about we meet some time for coffee. Do you know Murph's on Wilshire?"

The alarm sounded the next day at 6:15, and he threw on jeans and a sweater. Coming home from his walk the previous day he'd left a message at Murph's that he would meet Max outside Franklin Elementary the next day at seven. Downstairs at 6:30, he fixed breakfast of coffee, fruit and toast, considering an egg but deciding he didn't have time. For some reason, he was exhilarated. Normally, he didn't like early mornings which is why he kept his room dark and hated alarms, but he'd quite sprung out of bed like a boy again. Breakfast done, he cleaned up, grabbed his picker from the hall closet and left the house, carefully closing the door. Still no sign of Nancy. Outside, he picked up the paper, tossed it on the porch and started down the street. He'd gone half a block before he realized he hadn't even checked the headlines. News of the previous day's disasters, whatever it was, would have to wait.

Even from a distance, everything about Max was medium—medium height, medium build, medium clothes of medium colors, though the red of his bandana stood out. You might call him non-descript, except that Max had a presence. Even standing alone under a ficus tree leaning on his picker, he had an attitude, holding his instrument, not quite leaning on it, much as a gentleman with his stick, a certain elegance in the posture, a physical grace that said that this trash picker knew what he was about. Up close, the dark eyes behind the spectacles took you in, intense, interested, revealing nothing.

"Good morning," he said, pulling up his bandana. "I thought maybe we'd work up to San Vicente this morning. How's that sound?"

"Just lead the way."

The sun inched up as they went. It was already May, the sun in and out, the smoke not yet bad, the kind of day that might stay cool and help the firefighters. He watched Max maneuver his picker like a baton, darting here, grabbing there, artistry in every maneuver. Andy told himself to concentrate on the task, not on the master picker across the street and not on the scenery. Picking demanded discipline, eyes down, never up, sweeping the terrain. It was good work, environmentally positive, personally satisfying, challenging in that you didn't want to miss a thing, not even a tiny chewing gum wrapper trying to hide under a sycamore leaf.

They went down Alta to 14th, turned and headed north, staying on opposite sides, not communicating. At San Vicente, Max pointed, and they crossed to a large trash can. Emptying, Andy saw that Max's bag contained twice the trash as his own. Embarrassing, but if Max noticed, he said nothing. Back on the trail, they headed south to Georgina and turned east. It was more like exercising your dog than working. You couldn't ignore the dog, but apart from that just a long, easy walk. The dog gave you a purpose, made the walk something more than an idle stroll. His left wrist began to ache, and he switched hands. He was left-handed.

Back at Murph's, Agnes took their order.

"I'd like a three-minute egg with my bagel," Andy said.

"You got it."

"Need some protein, do you?" said Max.

"I wanted an egg at breakfast but didn't have time. You like eggs?"

"Don't eat eggs much anymore. Used to like them hard-boiled."

"I lived in France a while," Andy said. "Café like this with a counter always had a rack with hard-boiled eggs. Salt shaker nearby. I've never seen one in this country."

"Can't say I ever have either."

"You been abroad?"

"Mmm, you might say that."

If he had more to say on the subject, it was stopped by Agnes returning with the coffee and bagels. "Egg'll be right here," she said, lingering a moment, looking at him. "Everything all right, Max?" she asked.

She'd laid her hand on the table, and Max covered it with his own. "Fine, Agnes, fine."

It was an unusual gesture, and Andy looked closer. Agnes was nowhere near Max's age, but looked about as much older than she was as Max looked younger. She had a round, florid face and wore her hair in a chignon. He'd noticed something between them from the beginning, a connection, friendship, something more than waitress and customer.

"Pretty good day, Max, wouldn't you say?" he asked when she was gone.

"We did all right, yes."

"How do you know when it's time to stop. You don't wear a watch."

"Body tells me."

Agnes was back with the egg. "Three minutes on the dot," she said.

He knocked off the top with a spoon and cracked it in the cup, carefully scooping the white. Shook in salt and pepper and mixed it up. "Nothing better with coffee and a bagel."

"Can't argue with that."

He'd gotten out of the habit of simple places like Murph's and laconic people like Max. "What do you think Max? I mean about the situation we're in?"

"Which situation would that be?"

"The plague. The planet. The president."

He took off his glasses and rubbed his eyes. Put his glasses back on. "To tell you the truth, I don't think much about those things."

"But isn't that why you're out here—to do your part?"

He thought a moment. "I've been picking a lot longer than two of those things have been around."

"Well, *why?*"

He finished his bagel. "There you go with your whys again."

Agnes was back to fill their cups. "Anything else, Max?"

"Don't think so."

Andy examined his companion, who was looking out onto Wilshire. Murph's was a corner shop, giving a good view onto the street. "Seems to me the two things are related: what you do here on the streets and concern for the planet."

Max looked back. "Never thought of it like that."

"Then why are you out here every day?"

"I'll tell you something just to get you to stop asking: Let's say I believe in order."

"Order?"

"Harmony. Things in their places. Dynamic balance, you might call it."

"You talk in riddles."

"No riddle to it. You saw what I do. You joined me. We did the job. Now we're eating together. Where's the riddle?"

"The connection."

"Forget connections. Noesis ruins things. Go with the feeling."

"Noesis?"

"Over-thinking, let's say. You want to do something, just do it."

Chapter 8

Dear Andy,

Ah, Avenue Niel. It wasn't my first flat in Paris, I'd already had two others. Nobody seems to want to live in the 17th, but when I found it I loved it. I'd stayed with my aunt in the 16th at first, but that was too quiet even for me. Next was the Latin Quarter, across from the jazz place Chat qui Pêche, which was so noisy I left after two months. Then came the job at the hospital and the flat in the 17th. Yes, it was tiny, but it was quiet! It was over an épicerie and down the street from the caviste we came to know so well. Remember Monsieur Jules, the shop owner? The barrels, the wine bottles, the must, the gnats. The Auvergnat accent we couldn't understand. His wife's was not much better.

Paris life sticks in the mind, doesn't it? I shall never forget Jules and his little shop. He only had one table, and we were the only ones who ever sat down. The men would stand at the bar and toss off their petits rouges while we sat and watched. They were always sneaking looks at us, like to say, what a funny place for a date. The only other woman I ever saw Chez Jules was Mme. Jules. Sometimes she would see me coming home and ask me in for a nightcap. She looked after me, told me she worried when she didn't see me.

I have so much to say in response to your last, which moved me to tears. What if ... what if? Before replying, I need time to think, to sort things out. For me, that means, as you will remember, walking. I will get some exercise before the sun disappears into the Celtic Sea. I will walk down to the bay to watch the boats, try not to think of this horrible virus that is killing us. Though it is still mostly on the other side of the island, the government has ordered a curfew across the entire U.K. I don't see why they can't take a more targeted approach.

The ocean makes me think of you for some reason. By the way, when is your birthday? It would be so nice to send you a card. If only I had your home address.

Philippa

He'd had strange dreams the night before. They were outside Franklin Elementary, and Max was handing him a picker only instead of the picker with a gripper at the end, this one had a spike like the old-fashioned pickers he'd used in the army for policing, trash duty designed exclusively for privates. It was less a spike than a pike, and Max was handing it to him and telling him he'd know what to do with it. Then Elly showed up, or it might have been Philippa because she was wearing a skirt. He handed her the picker and she came at him like with a sword. Why would she do that? He woke up, soaking, felt almost like opening the window, but he never did that. His dreams, like his life, had become a riddle and a muddle.

Unrested, he went downstairs for breakfast, picking up the newspaper on the way and checking the garage. Nancy's car was missing. She'd not come home. He thought about it, thought about Chuck, a stab of anxiety passing as he headed back inside. He had no appetite for breakfast but made coffee and carried it with him into the den. On the computer he located Philippa's last letter, reading it several times, pausing finally over the last lines.

Should they exchange home addresses? Would Nancy object to his correspondence with an old girlfriend? Would *he* object if she started a correspondence with an old boyfriend? But Philippa was Paris. Nobody gets Paris out of the system. He'd written a novel about it and still hadn't got it all out, never would, he knew that. A movable feast, *non*? Everyone he'd known in Paris was dead, everyone but Philippa. The last connection. He needed her. This is what writers do. They hold on to things. Build on them. Why not home addresses? They could turn this into an old-fashioned correspondence by post. He wondered if England still had those red pillar post boxes he remembered. Philippa probably had beautiful handwriting, like all well-brought-up English girls. His was a scrawl, but he could brush it up. He needed to think about that.

> *Dear Philippa,*
>
> *It took us a while, didn't it? What I remember is that when you left me sitting alone on the Place des Ternes, I knew I'd never see you again. The last words you spoke before running for your bus were, "What am I doing in Paris?" I was certain you were gone for good, sick of Paris, sick of nursing, sick of married men, sick of me. I don't know how long I sat watching Bus 93s come and go and thinking I should get on, go out to the hospital, pull you out of recovery and tell you I loved you and would never*

let you leave me. Ridiculous, no? They'd have put me in the psychiatric ward. Or called the police. I think it was soon after that that Artie took me across the street to the bar in the Hotel California for another of our little chats.

But maybe not. He did that a few times, and each time I thought it was to fire me. When I ran into Artie years later in New York he told me he'd never seriously considered firing me. We'd bumped into each other on Fifth Avenue—he was working for the Voice of America—and we slipped into the bar at the St. Regis. He said I'd often been "a bit of a mess" but always managed to straighten up. It was the last time I saw him. Artie Schwartz was a mensch. Maybe not with everyone for he had his enemies. The new owners hated him because he wasn't one of theirs. He was what the sports guys call a players' coach. With me, he was the best. I don't think he ever knew about you, but one never knew for sure with Artie.

I gave up calling the hospital. I didn't know where you lived, just somewhere on Avenue Niel. I walked over there a few times hoping to catch you on the way to the bus, but never saw you. I dropped into Churchill's after work. No sign. Certain you'd gone back to England, I started feeling really stupid, like a high-schooler hanging around after class hoping to catch sight of some girl he had a crush on. I'd given up when one day I remembered the farmer's market in Levallois. You went there on market days, you said. I caught the 93, walked to the market and there you were, a pretty girl with a basket on her arm, like the Renoir painting.

As I sit here typing these words, that day comes flooding back—the sunshine, the colors, the calls from the stalls, the old ménagères elbowing to the front to squeeze melons before being shooed away, the sounds from the Seine and Seurat's Grande Jatte just down the street, you standing there looking at me for what seemed like hours before coming up and kissing me on the cheek. Do you remember? That's where it started for us. After all the stops and starts, the farmer's market in Levallois brought us togeth-er. We went to the Grande Jatte for lunch and later discovered Martin-Pêcheur, the fish-restaurant by the Ile de Puteaux. I thought Martin-Pêcheur was the owner's name until you told me it was a bird. How stupid I was in those days. But I'd found you again.

I've gone on too long. So easy to get lost in the past, safe harbor from the dismal present. And yes, I remember Mme. Jules. She was not the only one to worry when she didn't see you.

Andy

She was dressed again in tights, running shoes and tee shirts, this time with a red scarf covering her face. She slipped into the booth opposite him. He had the view of Wilshire; she had the view of him. Agnes came out from behind the count-er, staring at Andy, then at Elly. "You can take that off, honey, now that you're seated." He'd asked about Max when he ar-rived, and Agnes said he only came mornings. He wondered what he did the rest of the day. Having spent a good part of two days with Max, he knew almost nothing about the man.

"You want to look at the menu or you know what you want?" Agnes asked Elly.

"Can you make a parfait?"

"Sure, what kind?"

"How about yogurt, berries and granola? And a glass of water, please."

She wrote it down. "And you?"

"Grilled cheese on sourdough and coffee. No water."

"Make that two coffees," said Elly.

"You been running?"

"Afterward. Right now I need calories. And water. The smoke from the fires is bad today. I rarely head up this way. I didn't know places like this still existed."

"I come here sometimes for breakfast," he said, leaving out Max and his picking duties. "Murph's grows on you." He found he liked sitting there with an attractive young woman. It had been a while. So," he began, "how are you holding up? Things any better at home?"

Her silence gave him the answer.

"Look at it this way," he said. "This, too, will end."

"No, Mr. McKnight, things will never be the same again."

"They're talking of a vaccine."

She frowned. "That's not what I meant."

He knew what she meant. Agnes brought the coffees.

"Mr. McKnight ..."

"I'm a little older than you, Elly, but please call me Andy."

She nodded. "What I meant is that we will never recover from this, never, ever."

"Yes, the planet will not recover from our mistreatment of it. We are no longer worthy stewards."

Agnes was back with their order. He stared at the parfait thinking he would love to ask for a taste, but couldn't do it. He didn't like sweets, but it didn't look sweet. He took a bite of his grilled cheese, runny, but not too. Just right. Murph's was a good joint, a relic of the fifties that made it into the next century.

"We've lost four years," he said.

She finished a scoop and wiped her mouth. "That's not even what I meant. Just shows how selfish I've become. You were thinking of the planet. I was thinking of my own life."

He might have smiled at that, thinking it could have been Nancy. Instead, he sipped his coffee and waited. It was the journalist in him. Shut up and listen.

"Friends," she said. "I've lost friends and will never get them back. We can't talk anymore. Girls I've known all my life, gone to school with, played tennis with, sorority sisters. Girls I've been able to talk to about everything ... and I mean *everything*. Done. Forever. Gone." She paused and stared down at the parfait. "All because of *him*. You're a writer, Mr. McK ... sorry, Andy," she smiled, "it's hard to call you that, you know."

"You'll get used to it."

"I was going to say that you're a writer so you've studied these things, but have we ever had a president so full of hate? He spews hate in everything he says or does, and it spreads to everyone, even to people like me who've never hated anything."

She paused. "But I'm learning."

She'd opened her veins and was bleeding in front of him. What could he say? That it would soon be over? But she'd just said it would never be over. He knew that young people were suffering the most. Old folks like him were dying, but at least they were old. If they'd had dreams, they'd fulfilled them or lost them. The lives of Generation Z, girls like Elly, already stunted by the distortions of social media, were collapsing under the load of a depraved president and a plague that isolated them and deepened their addiction to the lies and fantasies of the internet. Anxiety had turned to depression, and now young people killed and maimed themselves if they didn't get enough "likes" on their Instagram page. He thought back on his own time at UCLA a half century before Elly. Nothing but good memories.

Agnes had been lingering and wandered over with the coffee pot as Elly worked on her parfait. "Very good," she told the waitress.

"Haven't seen you before," said Agnes. She refilled the cups and put down the check. "Be sure and come back. Long as we're open, that is. You never know anymore."

"I never thought," Elly went on when Agnes was gone, "that different views could ruin friendships. I'm only twenty, but it never happened before. I have friends who are religious, who are atheists, who are socialists, who have different views on women's rights, on sororities, on men, on drinking, on everything. We argue, we disagree. We have a few beers. We laugh. They're still my friends, my sisters. But I cannot ... will not ... associate with anyone who supports a man as racist ... as depraved ... as truly evil ... as Trump. Covid is a hoax, he says, just like climate change. Don't trust the scientists, he says, trust me. Don't worry about the environment, he says, look at the stock market. He cannot open his mouth without defiling someone or something. No, no, I'm sorry. I can't go that far." She paused for breath. Then: "What can we do?"

It wasn't anything he hadn't said a hundred times himself, but how much better to hear it from someone who was young and active and could do something about it. She had passion because her life had collapsed. His life hadn't collapsed. He had money, a house that was paid off, two cars, a country club he didn't use, all the amenities of the rich, idle, and old. This girl, on the other hand, was losing everything, starting with youth and hope. She was desperate for answers.

She looked abashed. "Here I am complaining about a selfish world, and I can't stop talking about myself."

He felt a gush of sympathy. He would love to have taken her hand, but that was a bad idea. He reminded himself that he could be her grandfather, though he'd never felt like anyone's grandfather. He wished they could switch seats so she would at least have something to look at besides him. There is something calming about watching passing street life, life going on despite the plagues, despite the masks, anonymous humanity living out its time.

"Go on, Elly."

"The worst part. My father. I told him how awful I thought Trump was acting during the pandemic, lying, denying, so afraid things will be blamed on him, criticizing doctors, criticizing scientists, criticizing reporters, holding rallies where people all around are falling sick and dying. We need someone who will take charge, I said."

She stopped, and her eyes fell as if she might not go on, might not want to tell him the rest of what she'd started to say. Suddenly she looked up, her eyes fixed steadily on him. "Dad said something that took my breath away. He said that the pandemic was mainly killing old and poor people and so maybe it was a good thing. Trump was right to let it alone, he said, to let some people get sick and die. Science did not have an answer for things like this. It was a kind of natural culling, natural selection." Her face was flushed, a mixture of shame and anger. "I'd never heard him say anything like that before. Never. *That's* what Trump has done to us."

It was likely the first time she'd told anyone what Sam Lancaster had said, and she was embarrassed. She'd been close to her father. He remembered the days when he and Nancy played doubles against Sam and Elly at the club. Even as a junior she could carry her father. Sam didn't mind. He was so proud of her. She did not like repeating his words, but she was angry.

"Sounds impossible, doesn't it? That a person like Trump could actually break up families. But I know of other stories. Apparently it's happening all over the country—fathers and daughters, mothers and sons, brothers and sisters, boyfriends and girlfriends, husbands and wives. Things happening that have never happened before. Half the country is caught in a kind of devil worship. What can we do?"

Agnes was back to make change, staring at Elly. She would have to be deaf not to have heard.

Chapter 9

He smelled the coffee as he came downstairs. At the beginning of life in this house he'd often smelled coffee as he
came down, but in recent years he'd been the coffee maker.
Nancy was a more nocturnal creature, and when she took up
bridge started staying out more, going to bed later and sleeping later. He was still at the *Times* in those days and when
on rewrite often didn't get home until after the first edition,
around eleven. On her bridge nights they sometimes arrived
home at the same time and would have a drink together before heading upstairs. He had given up bridge, but Nancy's
group often kept her up late so that he was the first one down
most mornings. He brought in the paper, made the coffee,
sometimes even was out on his walk before she was down.

Since they'd returned from Kauai things were out of
kilter. Something ominous about finding her down so early,
unnatural. She was still in her robe.

"Good morning," he said. "You're up early."

"Good morning."

"Bad night?"

"Bad night."

She looked it. One of the advantages of separate bedrooms is that it gives couples the chance to fix themselves up
before coming down, something recommended as you grow
older. Nancy had grown to like private morning time, and
rarely came down before she was ready. When she took care

she could look twenty years younger, almost the woman he'd met in the lingerie department of Robinson's. Most of the time she took care.

She'd set out coffee cups, oranges, milk, butter and the baguette from the Montana bakery he'd bought the night before. The coffee was brewing in the French press, and silently they waited. After a while, he sat down. Something was in the air besides the scent of coffee. When it was ready, she poured and sat down across from him. He tried a smile, but she didn't notice. She did not look good.

"Andy, once more: do you have anything to tell me?" Her voice was flat, tired, decisive.

He sipped and let the coffee do its work. Their eyes finally met. Her hair was stringy. His head dropped. He was not used to this.

"You want something," he said. "I don't know what it is."

She stared at him for some time. "You really don't, do you?"

"What is it that's bothering you? It can't still be dinner at the Godfreys."

"No."

"What then, for God's sake," he said, voice rising. "Let's not go on like this."

Still as a statue, she sat looking down into her coffee, only the faint sound of her breathing showing any signs of life.

Finally, very softly: "Philippa."

His head shot up so quickly that the nerve in his neck stabbed, shooting pain into his brain. He started out of his chair, grabbing at his neck before slumping back down. "Sorry," he said, "give me a minute."

The intense pain gave him a moment to catch his breath. He stared at her, shocked at the violation. He thought he knew his wife, the most honest, straight-forward, equitable person he had ever known. The idea that she would have gone into his computer to search his correspondence was unimaginable.

"I can't believe you would do that," he said.

"Do what?"

"Go into my computer."

"I didn't go into your computer."

He continued rubbing his neck, massaging the stinging nerve. As the pain gradually subsided, he thought—so what if she is reading my correspondence? He had nothing to hide. He'd have told her about it if he'd thought she would care. She knew what Paris meant to him. But the treachery of it, that he could not accept.

"I have nothing to hide from you, Nancy. Certainly not my correspondence with Philippa Grey, a woman I knew in Paris a half century ago. But the idea that you would go into my computer to read my letters is appalling. You've never done anything like that. Why would you do it now?"

It took her a while to answer. He'd never seen her like this, unkempt, dejected, but so determined. He had to look away.

"I did not go into your computer."

"Then how do you know about Philippa Grey?"

"You mean Philippa Hughes?"

He frowned. "If you prefer."

"Certainly not from you."

"Not from me and not from my computer. Are you clairvoyant?"

She looked up. "Don't, Andy. This is serious. Why didn't you tell me?"

"*Tell you?* Do you tell me about all your correspondence?"

She shook her head. "I would never have a correspondence like this."

"*Like this?* You say that as though there's something wrong with it. But there is nothing wrong with it—and I had no idea you'd be interested in my exchanges with an old girlfriend."

"She doesn't write like an old girlfriend."

"What do you mean?"

"Her husband has just died. She wants to resume with you."

"She's a seventy-five-year old grandmother, for heaven's sake." He tried some cold coffee to see if it would help his head. "How do you know about this, Nancy?"

"Your secret correspondence with Philippa Grey is on my computer. I don't want to read it, but it stares me in the face, and I do read it."

"Secret?"

"What else to call it?"

"How can it be on your computer?"

"Your messages were forwarded to my computer when we were in Kauai, remember? They still are."

"Why don't you delete them?"

"I have deleted them."

"Shouldn't you stop them being forwarded?"

"I have done that now."

"Why did you wait?"

"Oh, stop it, Andy! The issue isn't that I read these letters, but that they exist."

She hadn't taken a bite, nor had he. The cold coffee on his empty stomach plus his sore neck and the tension from this dreadful conversation made him nauseous. He broke some bread, ate it and went to the shelves for a glass. He needed milk to calm his stomach. He wasn't certain how to approach this. He was being accused of something he felt was natural and good, that made him happy in a time of trouble and misery, yet Nancy's reaction showed she took it in a manner he could never have imagined. He thought back on the letters. Two old lovers sharing memories of their time in Paris. How many tens—hundreds—of thousands of lovers have done it back to the Middle Ages? Paris does that.

"This has nothing to do with you, Nancy. I have reconnected with someone from my youth. When I wrote my book on Paris I looked for anyone I knew in those days. Most of them are dead."

"And Philippa?"

"I had no idea where to find her. I didn't look. She found my books in a bookstore in England and dropped me a line. She's not the first person to do that, you know."

"How many ex-girlfriends wrote you?"

"Well ..."

"You see how this is different, don't you?"

"No, frankly I don't."

"You loved this girl. She broke up your first marriage. You went with her how long, five six years?"

"Five years."

"She's still in love with you."

"And thirty-five with you."

"She's still in love with you!"

"Nonsense. We're reminiscing about our youth. You're allowed to do that at our age. Most of our life is in memories. You try to keep them alive."

"It is too much, Andy."

"What do you mean, too much?"

"Too much for me."

He started up. He wanted to come around and hug her, tell her to forget it, that nothing was changed between them, but she was up before him, retreating to the sink, standing there.

"Don't," she said. "I need more time to process this."

He sank back down, head aching, heart thumping. He wanted to make light of it; he was a writer at work, that's all there was to it, but she'd thrown him off the rails. He couldn't make light of something that was affecting her this much.

"I've been reading these letters for what, three weeks now," she said, "and thinking about them for just as long. They have made my life a misery. Your life is more in these letters than in this house; more with this woman than with me."

"That simply is not true."

"I believe it is true, and that's what matters. I've been waiting for days for you to tell me about this. That might have persuaded me that it was as incidental, as trivial, as you pretend, grist for some new book you had in mind, and you'd tell me about it as you always do with your new ideas. But you didn't. You didn't because you wanted to keep it a secret, because we have no communication anymore. The communication is all with this woman in England, and maybe with other people in your life that I know nothing about. What is the point in going on with a marriage in which we no longer share anything?"

It took a moment to digest her words, which clearly contained a threat. He was upset, angry, but pain and sympathy crowded in as well, confusing him. Finally, he shook his head. "I have to say that I am astounded by your reaction to this."

Her face flushed. "How dare you treat something like this so offhand, so casually. These letters are an arrow into my heart."

He saw the tears fall, and felt wretched. "I am so sorry."

The silence was crushing. He wanted up and away, to escape, out on the trail to breathe again but could not move. They'd never had a scene like this. He did not know how to stop it.

"You empty your heart to this woman. When have you ever done that with me?"

The injustice shocked him. "For thirty-five years." He would not be put in the dock for something so innocent.

"What did you tell me the other day? 'There is no us anymore.'"

"You took that completely wrong," he said, sympathy waning. "I was trying to say that in these terrible days of fire, disease, and death; when we're burdened with the most horrid president in history and a worthless Congress in a time of mortal danger, we can't afford to think of ourselves. We are losing time."

"Maybe you should spend less of it writing to old girlfriends."

The comment was so out of character that he felt suddenly afraid. She was pushing this to the point of no return, and she knew it. She stood there defiantly against the sink, arms folded, staring not at him but at the table with the untouched food. What motivated her—anger, jealousy, fear? How could she so completely misunderstand his desire to escape the poison of a defiled and dying world into the comforts of memory?

"Are you telling me to whom I can write?"

"What are you going to do about it?"

"Are you asking me to stop writing to her?"

Her eyes were hard, and they fixed on him without blinking. She didn't want to move, but her fidgety hands gave away the turmoil going on inside. Neither of them quite grasped what was happening, but they plunged ahead anyway. Would it have been easier if he had told her? Was it something about finding it on her computer? If she'd found letters from England in the mailbox would that have made it any easier?

But that wouldn't have happened, would it? It was the computer that made such correspondence possible, the instant exchange of reminisces and affections as though you are in the same house, the same room, the same bed. You can't do that with letters that take weeks to arrive.

He wished he hadn't put the question so starkly, but he had, and she would not dodge it, though she was trapped. To answer yes was to lose the fight because if he didn't abandon the correspondence voluntarily it was meaningless. To answer no was to condone something that had brought her to the breaking point. She had to answer no. Anything else would be unacceptable to both of them.

What he should have known, at least sensed, was that the correspondence had brought to a boil something simmering since Kauai—at least since Kauai because that's why they'd gone there. She had come to believe that she couldn't live with him anymore, that his obsession with the two plagues had become too much for her.

And unlike many unhappy spouses of her age and predicament, Nancy had options.

"No," she said. "That is a decision you'll have to make for yourself."

"Thank you."

"I'm going up for a bath, Andy. You'll have to have breakfast by yourself—which I'm sure you won't mind."

He sat there for some time, listening to the bath running, knowing she'd be upstairs most of the morning, waiting for him to be gone. He put the food away and stood a moment looking out the window into the backyard. It was just eight o'clock, and the sun had not yet quite made it above the pines behind the house.

What a way to start the day!

He opened the kitchen door and stepped outside for fresh air, but smelled only smoke. Spring fires once were rare because the forests stayed soaked from winter rains. Fires in the mountains are normally autumnal, when brush and trees dry out from long, hot summers. But there was no normal anymore. The West Coast had fires all year because it was dry all year. The Gulf Coast had hurricanes all year because it was wet all year. Everything was topsy-turvy. He looked out over his backyard, ratty because of water restrictions. Some neighbors had replaced lawns with plastic grass. Or cactus. Careful where you step.

He knew he should eat something but had no appetite. Crisis in the morning can ruin the best of days. Looking at his poor lawn, he found himself thinking of Seurat's lawn painting of la Grande Jatte, so perfect, so elegant, children playing, lovers loving, men in high hats, women with parasols. And the colors, oh, the colors! How did he create those vibrant reds, greens and blues just using thousands of tiny dots? The little Paris island wasn't like that anymore, or at least wasn't like that when he was there with Philippa. Seurat's lawns were replaced by the concrete of sidewalks and buildings. But the *péniches*, the old barges that once plied the Seine were still there, transformed into homes moored permanently to the island, decks now covered in plants and flowers like a country cottage. The scenes were so vivid in his mind that he wanted to write Philippa about it, remind her of how it had been. He could not. Reality hung too heavy on his mind. Escape on this day would be impossible.

He went to the hall closet, took out the picker and shoulder bag, grabbed his scarf and hat and set out. Max would be out there somewhere, but he would never find him in the labyrinth of Santa Monica neighborhood streets. But maybe he didn't need Max. He'd spent six hours with him as an apprentice picker. He was ready to strike out on his own.

Chapter 10

He was already seated and ready to order when Max came in. The old man stood over him a moment, staring down at the bag and picker as he pulled down his bandana, his leathery skin meticulously shaven as always. Andy felt his spirits lift. He badly needed company.

"I take it that empty bag has been full," Max said, putting his things down and sliding into the booth.

"Yes."

"The cub has found its legs."

"Cub still needs papa bear. We need to fix a place to meet."

"Murph's is the place. I drop off my bike just before seven. Back at ten."

"Every day?"

"These days."

"I started at eight," Andy said. "Where were you then?"

"I never know where I'll be at eight. Sometimes I do south of Wilshire. Follow my nose." He paused. "And then, I have other work."

He was about to ask about the "other work" when Agnes came up with two cups of coffee. "Bagels and one three-minute egg?"

"No egg today," said Andy.

"Filled the bag," Max said when Agnes was gone. "That's good."

"How about you?"

"Two bags full."

"Baa, baa, black sheep."

"That was three bags."

Their eyes met, and they chuckled. Max seemed too exotic to know an old English nursery rhyme. They were still smiling as Agnes came back with the bagels. "What's so funny?"

"We're doing nursery rhymes," said Max.

"Entering second childhood are you?"

"Why not? The first one was no good."

The coffee felt good, driving away the thought of the cold coffee that nauseated him earlier, though it wasn't just the coffee. He studied Max, who was looking out on Wilshire. Everything about him seemed slow, how he moved, how he talked, how he ate his bagel, even how his eyes moved, strangely with the head.

"What did you mean about your first childhood, Max?"

The head turned, but the owl-eyes did not look directly at him, but to the side. "You are an inquisitive type, aren't you?"

"Lifetime of practice."

"Well," he started and stopped, his gaze shifting back to Wilshire. He was deciding. "Well," he resumed, "I was going to say that maybe if we're going to work together it's not a bad idea to get to know each other. You say you're a writer, that it?"

"I was a writer all my life. I'm an old guy now, but old habits die hard."

"They do, don't they?"

"You're an unusual man, Max."

"Because I like to clean streets?"

He wished he had the Wilshire view, but that was Max's seat. He looked to the rear, couple of empty booths, another with two elderly women in hats, masks at their necks. Three

guys at the counter, one table with a couple having late breakfast, painted signs at the rear said toilets and exit, one yellow
neon Coors sign. How many hundreds of little joints were
there around the country like Murph's—thousands, tens
of thousands? Every country has its own unique hangouts
and he'd been in them all—English pubs and teashops, U.S.
bars and diners, French cafes and bistros, German Kneipes,
Spanish bodegas, Italian bars and trattorias, on and on, all
with different looks and smells and characters reflecting
local tastes and routines and cultures. Would any of them
survive the plague? How different would the new world order be? Some shops along Santa Monica streets already had
shuttered. He wondered about Murph's. Was there a Murph
or was it just a name?

"That's part of it," Andy said, returning to the present.
"You mentioned other work. What else do you do?"

Gazing out at Wilshire, it took him a while to answer. "Ah,
well, let me ask *you* a question: What is your full name?"

"McKnight, Andrew Stewart McKnight."

"English?"

"Scottish. Originally Mac Neachtain, but nobody could
pronounce it."

"It means son of the knight, I believe."

"Something like that."

"You spent time in Europe?"

"A dozen years or so."

"Any languages?"

"Picked up some."

"German?"

"Some German, yes,"

"My name is Maxim Erbsenhaut. Do you know what
Erbsenhaut means?"

Of course, he knew. Erbsen and Haut are two common German words, but what was he getting at? "I do know those words."

"Pea skin. I am Max Pea Skin."

He read the puzzled look on Andy's face. "I see you can also ask questions without using words. "I will answer the question on your face and in so doing will answer your original question, which had to do with my first childhood."

They'd finished their second cup by the time he got to the end of the story. He was born in Kyiv, Western Ukraine, in 1934. Decades earlier, the family came up from the south to settle near Lviv, in Galicia, which is mining country. His father, a furrier, was son of a rabbi, who was son of a miner, who was a son of another miner. They had Jewish names when they arrived, foreign names that nobody could pronounce. Like your family with Mac Neachtain, he said. As Galicia was part of the Austro-Hungarian Empire, they were given German names. The list of names given to Galician Jews fills books, and some of them, like Erbsenhaut, were meant to be ridiculous, to label you as outsiders, as Jews. Erbsenhaut is not so bad in English, he said, because nobody knows what it means.

His parents survived Stalin's genocide, which killed four million Ukrainians, but their luck ran out in '41 during Hitler's first trip into Soviet Russia. They were part of the 100,000 Kyiv Jews murdered at Babi Yar in September of that year by the Germans. Young Max was luckier. He'd been sent to live with his uncle Max, also a furrier, in Lviv. His uncle, along with his aunt and young Max, escaped through Romania to Greece and eventually Lisbon and New York. In New York they made money. Women wore furs in those days. They kept their name.

He smiled to break the tension. "So you see, young man, some childhoods are better than others."

"I love the young man, Max. I was born in 1941."

"I'm glad something good happened in that terrible year."

"Terrible years are something I want to talk about."

"Never satisfied, are you?"

"It is my primary failing."

"And a serious one, I might add."

"Why do you say that?"

"It suggests acquisitiveness."

"I'm not looking for possessions. I'm looking for answers."

"Inquisitiveness, not acquisitiveness. I stand corrected."

"We are living through a terrible time. The worst in my memory."

Max, resolutely: "But not the worst in mine."

"It will turn out to be worse if we don't do something."

"Oh?"

"Hitler came to power because German conservatives thought they could use him to serve their own interests. Instead, he used them. When they finally woke up, it was too late. You don't see a lesson in that?"

The owl eyes ran across him and out to Wilshire. Andy watched the two ladies in hats get up and head for the counter to pay, carefully putting their masks back in place. They were well dressed in dark dresses with long sweaters and frilly collars, shopping clothes, though the hats were unusual for Santa Monica. The men at the counter had been replaced by others and with a young woman likely on a coffee break from one of the Wilshire shops still open. People came and went, but the nice thing about Murph's was the quiet. People talked, but kept their voices low, just for the person with them. Murph's was a place for nursing private thoughts.

Agnes was at the cash register for the two shopping women. Man looking out from the kitchen with the toque would be the cook. Maybe Murph.

Max's long face, seamed like the Galician mines where his forbears had worked, turned back to him, the rimless glasses illuminating his somber eyes. "Yes, I do."

Instead of explaining, he was laying down five dollars and motioning for Agnes. "We will save that conversation for another day. I have meetings to attend. Good bye."

Walking back along 23ʳᵈ Street, he found himself puzzled by the abrupt departure. With whom would an old street picker be meeting? From the beginning he'd sensed that Max was a soulmate, but it was tough to get him going. He'd finally opened up only to abruptly shut down again, frustratingly secretive. It was Friday, and he wouldn't see him again until Monday when they agreed to meet outside Franklin Elementary at the usual time.

He was just coming up on Franklin, which in normal times would be buzzing with playground shouts but was shut up like a mausoleum. The sun was gone, shrouded in clouds, fog and smoke—smog, the old curse of Los Angeles. He'd folded up his picker and was annoyed when he saw a plastic bag blowing along the street. He hurried to catch up with it, unfolded the picker, grabbed the bag and stuffed it in his bag. He laughed at himself. So this was how it was to be. No piece of trash shall remain un-bagged.

Nancy was gone when he reached home. She'd left a letter on the kitchen table. It was written on her powder blue stationery, lightly perfumed.

> *Dear Andy,*
>   *I've decided to move out for a while. How long,*
> *I don't know. I've taken a few things, but will have*

to come by to pick up things I'll need. We both need time to sort this thing out. Our life with each other has become intolerable. I hadn't told you, but I've begun to see a counselor to try to make sense of things. She thinks the decision to move out is the best thing for me, at least for now. I have purposely not told you where I will be. We'll run into each other from time to time, but please don't question me or try to find me. I'm sorry.

Love, Nancy

Numb, he sat there for some time, turning the letter over in his hand, inhaling its perfume, his thoughts returning to earlier times, better times. At length he stood, walked to the window and looked into the yard, listening to the silence. He stood there for minutes, not moving, not a twitch, waiting for some sound to bring him back to life, like a touch from Tinker Bell's wand. But there was nothing. It was a noiseless day, not a sound from house, street or yard. No bird, dog or child lifting its voice. Emptiness.

Eventually, the refrigerator started up, and he was freed. Listless, he went down the hall, glanced into his den, made a tour of the living room and started upstairs. He ignored his bedroom, looked into the guest room that had not had a guest since well before the plague, and turned into Nancy's room. He saw no sign of hurry, no disorder, everything in its meticulous place as always, the walk-in closet shut, the dresser drawers closed, the bathroom immaculate, like she was out for the day. He sat down on her bed, a bed he'd once used as much as his own, and was overcome by a feeling of immense sadness. He had lived with her in this house for thirty-five years and she was gone, warning him not to come after her.

It was her house. She had found it, not through a realtor but by deciding where she wanted to live and driving the streets until she had what she wanted. In the meantime, they lived in his Westwood apartment. It was 1979, oil was embargoed by OPEC, the dollar and economy shaky, and they settled on Santa Monica as a town that was still affordable and was on the Wilshire bus lines they both used to get to work without driving. There were communities closer to work, but he wanted to be near the ocean, and she dreamed of joining a country club. It took her weeks of searching. The houses she liked never had for-sale signs. The ones that did, she didn't like. One day there was a sign in front of a handsome Tudor place under the pines of 22nd Street. She met with the realtor the next day.

He knew those streets. As a boy he'd been raised a few miles to the south, but in those days the coastal towns all ran together: Malibu, Santa Monica, Ocean Park, Venice, Playa del Rey, El Segundo, Manhattan, Hermosa, Redondo. He swam at every beach. No trouble parking, no pollution, no masks, nothing to pay. While at UCLA he'd lived a year at Malibu. Four guys in a house on the beach for $800 a month. Imagine that in a place where $800 wouldn't buy you one night today. He knew the area where Nancy was looking because as a boy he'd driven there for weekly piano lessons with Robert Turner, the Santa Monica maestro. He hadn't been good enough for Turner, and it hadn't lasted. When they first arrived on 22nd Street he'd gone looking for the Turner house. He thought he found it one day, but when he knocked the lady said she didn't know anything about those days. Wasn't even born, she said.

Those were the fifties. The nation had come through a terrible depression and a terrible war and recovered. People didn't earn too much, but things didn't cost too much. If they did earn too much, a marginal tax rate of 90 percent assured they would share it. Dwight Eisenhower, a good and honorable man, won in two landslides and the nation stood tall, respected by everyone. Nobody thought about waste, plastic, fires, trolls, bots, liars, plagues, or the death of the planet. We faced dangers and met them. We made mistakes and corrected them. We had problems and solved them. We had good leaders and bad ones, but never a nasty, incompetent, dishonest humbug who came along at the absolute worst time, when the planet was diseased and on fire and gasping for help.

Feeling empty, he went downstairs and out into the backyard. A couple of wrens were bouncing around and pecking. Noise from children playing in the yard on 23rd drifted over the fence, familiar sounds to ease him back from his gloom. Inside again, he took up Nancy's letter and reread it. Hard to believe she wouldn't be coming in the front door any moment with a big hello and a kiss and a bag of groceries. He felt a chill, looked down, his hands were shaking, like he had a fever.

Dread. They'd reached the breaking point, the point where they made each other miserable, or, more accurately, where he made her miserable, and her misery increased his own. Awful as it was, it would be worse if she'd been there. They'd become strangers in their own house. He knew whose fault it was. She'd warned him often enough. But what was he to do? Nothing was right anymore.

Part Two

Chapter 11

In Paris, there'd been another kitchen, a tiny one in a flat that in its entirety was not that much larger than his Santa Monica kitchen. Paris junior flats often don't have full kitchens because they've been carved, like so many monks' cells, out of apartments that once stretched through the building front to back. A floor that once held two large flats could be made to hold a half dozen cubicles. The first room to disappear would be the kitchen, which became a partitioned part of the sitting area, which was also used for dining. The bed typically was behind another partition, or *cloison,* though it could just as easily be a daybed in the living area. Toilets and tiny showers would be somewhere, though often were in the hallway to be shared by others on the floor. Today, one finds stately nineteenth-century sandstone buildings from the Haussmann era, structures with ten-foot high solid oak front doors, wrought iron grills on the balconies and plaques of the famous on the facade, that inside are little more than tenements.

Entering her flat was like entering a gypsy salon for a palm-reading. A round table with dark velvet skirt and candles occupied the center of the room. Running the length of one wall was a dark sofa covered in bright throws and cushions. Scarlet ceiling-to-floor drapes hung on two sides, and the third was marked by an opening to a kitchenette and bathroom on one side and a narrow bedroom on the other. Most peculiar about the main room was its dimensions.

Though the floor of the building had been divided up horizontally to make cubicles, vertically the walls were as high as ever, giving the interior a nave-like feeling and making it impossible to heat. There were no visible windows, thus the drapes. All light was from lamps or candles.

"You do what you can with what you find," she said, watching him examine the room for the first time. "Splashes of color to brighten the gloom."

"Do you have something against daylight?"

"I have something against empty walls."

"I know there's a kitchen somewhere because I smell something."

"Blanquette de veau. I hope you're hungry."

He handed her the bottle of Brouilly he'd picked up along the Avenue Niel.

"You found my little caviste?"

"Chez Jules?"

"That's it."

"I didn't know what to get. Beaujolais works with everything."

"It will be fine with the blanquette. Come, I'll give you the five-second tour I give all first-time visitors."

There'd been times when he wondered if he'd ever see her again, let alone be invited to dinner; so many disruptions for so long that he'd come close to giving up. Guilt on both sides had not made it easier, nor had working nights. Philippa had a doctor boyfriend, and he, Andy, had a French wife. Add to that a certain shyness in both parties, whereas two bolder lovers might have plunged hard ahead. He'd gambled by tracking her down at the farmers' market, but she liked that. "A girl admires a certain persistence," she said in her English way. She'd left him standing on Paris streets three times, yet here he was.

When he left her nest the next morning the spell had been cast, and it never really broke. Events interfered and bad decisions were made, but the romance kindled that night lasted until he was pulled away from Paris, and she was gone when he returned. Fate's interventions can leave you gasping. He'd had a college friend at UCLA commissioned in the Navy who came home on leave one Christmas and by chance ran into a girl he'd dated in high school. They reconnected and fell in love, but she was engaged and he went back to duty. After exchanging a few letters he asked her to marry him. While awaiting her answer, he was transferred once, twice, three times. She answered yes and broke her engagement. He never got the letter. She married the man she'd rejected, who eventually committed suicide. When he saw her years later at another high school reunion she wouldn't speak to him.

Marriage between the French and English joins the world's oldest rivals, the ultimate frenemies, always have been and always will be. They marry, as Philippa's parents had married, but not often and often not successfully. Culturally, psychologically, and socially the French and English are different enough that wedded bliss defies all probability. The children of such marriages tend to do better because their Anglo-French genes are mixed rather than immiscible, as with the parents. To do better, however, the children must survive the often difficult relationship between the parents.

From her French mother she'd inherited not only her dark beauty, for she came to show him many family photos, but a gentle stoicism that carried her through the dramas of life. Stoicism didn't mean you accepted everything, just that you resisted only so far and then preferred to bend rather than break. From her mother, she also inherited her passion for nature. She was an outdoorsy person, who in her girlhood thought she might end up a squire's wife on some Midlands estate. Born of the privileged class, she was brought up in country houses and manors and learned to love dogs and horses, especially horses, fitting because that's what the name Philippa means. It is said that girls who love horses also love sex, and he had no reason to disagree, though it took some coaxing. From her mother she also inherited a love of literature, both French and English, and more than once said she was attracted to him and away from doctors and hospitals because he was a writer. But she was squeamish, which also gave him an edge.

She didn't talk much about her father, a professor of philosophy at Bristol. "Distrait" was the word she used, likely a good description for many philosophy professors. Her parents had met as the war broke out, one of those occasional moments in Franco-British history when they were on the same side, at least for a while, for reasons of survival. She was brought up in English girls' schools, learning the arts of being comely, polite, and unobtrusive, qualities most sought after by wellborn men of those times. Despite her French mother, English was always her first language. Even when they were away from the professor, they spoke only English. She would never have come to France to try her luck in the British Hospital had her mother's sister not married a Parisian and settled down in the luxury of a Passy apartment, one in which Andy McKnight would one day have the good fortune to spend a memorable afternoon.

Dear Andy,

I sit here in this big empty Devon house looking out on the Channel, but my mind is on the Seine. You mentioned Martin-Pêcheur, that wonderful barge-restaurant you found that we made our home away from home. I can't remember how you found it, someone on the newspaper, wasn't it? Of all our secret little Paris places, it was my favorite. Nearly invisible because of trees and the steep bank, you had to find the old winding stairway and start down without quite knowing where you would end up. Fish stew and oysters in season and Muscadet. And moules, which I liked more for the fun of eating them than for the taste. Sundays were best and then back to my little place on Avenue Niel.

Remember the time—how could I ever forget?— when we went back to my Aunt's flat on the rue de Passy. She was off in the south of France and had given me the key. I wonder if she'd have done that had she known I had a boyfriend. Aunt Clotilde was quite straight-laced, much more than her sister, my mother. She'd been a widow for so long she'd probably forgotten about men. That's not nice and I should strike it out but I won't because it's quite true. I remember it was a Sunday. I remember thinking how naughty I was to invite you there, but I couldn't resist. After all those times crammed in my little bed on Avenue Niel I wanted to get you in her big king-sized bed. I won't go into that anymore because I am blushing, and you may not even remember. If you do, tell me what you remember.

I was so naive. I knew almost nothing about that sort of thing. It's you who taught me, and I remember trembling sometimes while awaiting you, trembling with anticipation, with excitement. That's why I brought you to the rue de Passy. I kept thinking what it would be like with you on the fifth floor with a view out over the rooftops of Passy in Aunt Clotilde's king-

sized bed. I tried to convince myself it was wrong, that there probably hadn't been a man in that bed in fifty years, but I couldn't really find anything wrong with it. We never went back, so something must have bothered me. I think maybe I was trying to get even with all the family clucking and tut-tutting that had gone on around me as a girl, disapproving of this, warning of that, making sure I always dressed and acted properly and never spoke out of turn. Life was not fun but endless rules! I seem to remember thoughts like that running through my head that afternoon in Aunt Clotilde's bed: If they could just see me now! I suppose men don't have silly thoughts like that. Please tell me if I'm making sense.

You've told me very little of your present life. It must be hard to be American these days, even harder than to be a Brit. Boris Johnson is a clown and always has been, but nothing compared to your Trump. I see where he says that Covid will disappear like a miracle. Can he really believe that? Do you have any idea who the Democrats will put forward? Or maybe it doesn't matter since Trump is so thoroughly awful that he will lose to anybody. Are you going to be involved in defeating him? I hope so. I remember you as always being so passionate about politics. You loved your work so. It's you who told me the words of André Gide that I have never forgotten: "travail: opium unique."

Funny, that's something Aunt Clotilde might have said. Still, it is so true. We must keep going, despite everything.

Love, Philippa

He sat staring at the words for some time. Of course they'd loved each other, how could they not? They were young. It was Paris. Love was in the air. It was different for each of them, he knew that, more emotional for her, more physical for him. Nothing strange about it. They never talked about love; you don't do that at twenty-five. You just make it.

He crossed to the daybed to lie back and think it over. Why would she do that, suddenly do that? Did she possibly think ... ? Impossible. Love at the end of a letter is meaningless. Like Dear at the beginning. Nancy signed off with Love to almost anybody. He couldn't do that, but others did it without thinking. But to suddenly do it after—how many letters had there been? He went back over them. It was her fifth. Why now? Why just as he was losing his second wife?

The letter aroused him. He went into the kitchen for a glass of cold water. Did he remember the rue de Passy? How could he ever forget? The surprise was that she remembered it, an afternoon lifted straight from *Les Liaisons Dangereuses*. He suspected it was not the first such afternoon spent at that address, though not by the very proper Aunt Clotilde nor by her not quite so proper niece. Rue de Passy was a favorite site for eighteenth-century French aristocracy as it awaited the chopping of heads. He'd been the lucky recipient of her determination to get even with the repressions of youth. He'd been astounded by the vigor of her passion that afternoon. Such a proper little nurse. Finally, she could let go.

Part of it, he came to understand, was that her mind became synchronized with her body that afternoon. Physical lust comes and goes, but married to emotions like spite and revenge—*just look at me now!*—the body finds new energies. That was the genius of *Les Liaisons*, what lifted it above just one more story of Parisian licentiousness. The motivations behind the seductions of the Marquise de Merteuil and the Vicomte de Valmont were so exquisitely perverse that they lifted debauchery into the realm of art.

He went back to the computer to read over the letter again. She'd never quite opened up like that before, baring so much in so few paragraphs, letting go, just as she had that Sunday on the rue de Passy. He wondered if signing off with "love" had been unconscious, something flowing naturally from the content, scarcely noticed. He loved seeing the word. Yes, he would use it himself. He did love the girl. Or had. Or did. He wasn't sure.

His eyes came to rest on two other sentences: "Trump is so thoroughly awful that he will lose to anybody."

Would he lose to anybody? Had Americans finally had enough? Then how to explain the broken friendships, marriages, families; the shootings, riots, MAGA hats? The terrible truth was that his lies were succeeding. Maybe not with everybody, but with just enough people to steal another election. "The liar," Hannah Arendt wrote somewhere, "has the great advantage of knowing beforehand what the audience wants or expects to hear." Trump's lies, repeated daily, hourly, by Murdoch and his venal media machine and sent around the world on internet sites where lies are celebrated, made it more than possible that he could win again.

Then: "Are you going to be involved in defeating him?"

She sensed his powerlessness and frustration.

Chapter 12

He knew where Nancy had gone. They'd played bridge with Chuck and Ethel Collins in the old days, and even before Ethel died Chuck had eyes for Nancy. Chuck was a few years younger, but looked older so what did it matter. He was an aeronautical guy who worked somewhere in the Valley, the kind of big, pudgy, slow-moving type that plays bridge and dances and doesn't read the newspaper and that women like and men don't mind. Chuck's attentions to Nancy weren't a problem because Ethel would never have allowed him to step out of line. They were convivial bridge partners that unlike some of Nancy's grimmer friends didn't take the game so seriously that you couldn't have a few drinks and a few laughs while playing. They lived in Brentwood on a cul de sac he could never find, a few blocks up from Marilyn Monroe's old house. The last time he'd been there was for the repast after Ethel's funeral.

It's not good when your wife goes off with another man no matter how much you understand the reasons. The first instinct is to do something about it. Reason battles emotion until you understand that nothing can be done. Marriage is not a prison; the inmates are free to come and go. Even when reason wins out, the pain remains. They'd had the good steady relationship of two professionals who'd married late for love and companionship with no thoughts of leaving work or having children. When Nancy was promoted to buyer at

Robinson's she made more than he did at the *Times,* incomes they needed for the house on 22nd Street, which did not come cheap. From then on, they'd hardly had a quarrel. Things only started to go wrong in 2017. After that, disintegration was steady as the Trump poison spread across the country, seeping into households, setting quiet families against each other for the first time.

He brooded. The impulse to get in the car and find Chuck's house never left him, but the problem was what to do when he got there? He had a vision of Chuck politely going off to putter in his garage while he and Nancy faced off in the living room. The scene was ridiculous. She was a free woman. He was not a supplicant. What's more, nothing had changed. She would not be back in the house a day before she flew away again, this time surely for good. No, let matters take their course until she came back for the things she needed. They would meet each other in their own home and see if they were ready for a new start.

At least the crypt-like atmosphere after she discovered the letters was over. He knew she'd been thinking of separation before that, which is why they'd gone off to Kauai. Then came the incident at the Godfreys because he shouldn't have gone, but neither could he refuse her. But to go overboard over correspondence with a 75-year-old grandma he hadn't seen in half a century was madness. She would see that in time. Maybe her counselor would help her. Nothing had changed between them. What had changed was the slow asphyxiation of nation and planet. His work was to help her and everyone else open their eyes. *Opium unique.*

Max was not outside Franklin School the following Monday. He waited half an hour, but he never came. He'd said something about meetings the previous week, so maybe something had come up. Erecting his picker, he set out along Montana on his own, heading east, not west. He wasn't sure of the trashcans in that direction, but if they were on lower Montana they should be on upper. He would go up to Stanford and work the cross streets between Montana and Washington on the way back down. He would get to Murph's at ten to see if Max came.

Arriving, he spoke to Agnes and took the seat looking out on Wilshire, Max's seat. He ordered coffee, a three-minute egg and a bagel. Agnes had not seen Max, which was unusual. Mondays he was as regular as the clock on the wall, she said. He put Max out of his mind and tried to enjoy breakfast. Hours on the trash trail gives a man an appetite. He'd spent most of his life working for morning newspapers, which usually meant staying up late and sleeping late. He wasn't used to early mornings. He wasn't young anymore, not even middle-aged apparently, though he felt better than he had in his sixties. He wondered how Max did it. So many things to learn about the man. Strangely, he'd had no response at their last meeting when Hitler was mentioned, though everything in his life had been changed because of that man. "Save that conversation for another day," was all he said.

Eating slowly, in no hurry because nowhere to go and nothing to do, he watched the comings and goings on Wilshire. Something surreal about a world of masked people. Who was old, who was young? Who was handsome, who was ugly? With people dressing more alike, who was man, who was woman? Think of people who'd spent their lives worrying about their looks: weak chin, bad mouth, acne, scars, warts, big nose, small nose, people obsessing about one facial imperfection or another. Were they happier now that they could hide behind a mask? The phantom of the opera is no longer disfigured when everyone is masked.

Idle, silly thoughts for a man with nothing better to do. He was ready to go when he spied Elly Lancaster coming along Wilshire and waving. He recognized her green scarf and running clothes. And how she moved, gracefully, athletically. His spirits picked up.

"I took a chance," she said, dropping the scarf, smiling and slipping into the booth opposite him. "You said you came here for breakfast and here you are."

He was happy to stay. She ordered coffee and a bagel. He had a refill.

"You on a run?"

"Actually, I walked. I'm going up to Will Rogers to run the trail this afternoon."

"I've never been a runner. More of a swimmer."

"Pool or ocean?"

"Ocean as long as it's warm enough."

"There's always wetsuits."

"Wetsuits are for surfers."

Agnes brought the coffee and bagel.

"They have swimming wetsuits. Neoprene."

"I sometimes use a neoprene jacket. That's all."

He watched her bite into a bagel, something in her reminding him of Philippa. The hair was shorter, but the same jet black, same facial shape sans quite so prominent pommettes. The eyes and mouth were closest, the eyes slightly hooded, the mouth nearly identical, upper lip the perfect arc of a bow. Like Philippa, her lips remained slightly open in repose, as though there was something she wanted to say, as there clearly was. It's why she had come.

"How are things?" he asked.

She took a sip of coffee and dabbed at her mouth. "Bad."

"Sorry."

"It shows, doesn't it?" She sighed. "It's come to this: I have to move out. I wouldn't still be home anyway without the virus. I thought of the sorority, but it's closed."

"You and Sam aren't talking?"

"It's even worse with my mother. She takes his side in everything. We spend our time avoiding each other, like someone has the virus, which we don't."

"I've heard a few stories like that."

"You know, Mr. McK ... sorry, Andy, I have to talk about this to someone. *In person.* I'm sick of messages, tweets, posts, likes, unlikes. I'm sick of no classes, no professors, no face-to-face talks about what's happening to our country. I really enjoyed our talk the other day—enjoyed sitting here with you, like it was normal times. Which it isn't. So here I am again." She tried a smile. "I hope you don't mind."

"Of course, I don't mind. I enjoyed our talk as much as you did. We have an election in a few months." He thought of Philippa's letter. "We have work to do."

She was staring down into her cup, scarcely listening. "The latest fight came when Daddy said something about me lightening up, and suddenly I couldn't take it anymore. The nerve! The condescension! I said the whole mess was his fault, that his generation was destroying the planet *and just didn't give a damn.* They'd vote for Trump again for their portfolios and hopes of getting rid of all the dark faces, but the whole lot of them would be gone when the planet died, and I would be too. The grandchildren and their children would be screaming how could they have done this to us? Why didn't someone stop them?"

She didn't seem to notice that he belonged to her father's generation and maybe even one before that, but he wasn't going to argue, wasn't going to stop her. He wanted to hear everything she had to say. It was one thing for an old guy to have existential angst, so much better when young people who could do something felt it. He had to keep her going, help her spread it.

"Science gives us a decade to transition to renewables," she said, solemnly, "two decades to get to zero carbon to keep warming under 1.5 degrees Celsius. That's no time at all. We've lost four years under this horrible man so how can anybody lighten up?"

"And if we don't make it?"

"We enter the apocalypse zone."

She was eating and talking and taking sips in between to clear her throat. He was completely captivated. He'd read about the youth climate movement, dozens of grassroots groups determined to take power away from the Kochs and Exxons and hedge funds and start doing things themselves. The first step was to dump Trump. Most amazing about Elly, he thought, was that she was the daughter of Sam Lancaster, who taught the antediluvian economics of von Mises, Hayek, and Friedman. Maybe evolution was working after all.

"Listening to you, Elly, gives me hope. God knows, I could use a little."

"The trouble is," she said, "I don't know what to do about it. Nobody is meeting anymore, and I'm stuck in a house with parents I can't talk to. I'm twenty years old, for heaven's sake. Why am I still stuck at home? Why can't I do something?"

He looked up as Agnes refilled the cups. She smiled at Elly, who smiled back.

She was so attractive, so passionately engaged. How thrilling it must be to have a daughter like this, he thought, someone you could turn the planet over to; someone to trust to take things in hand. He'd never had children and never regretted it. In Paris it wasn't going to happen and with Nancy was too late to happen. Plenty of other people out there to replenish the population. Too many, really. But how wonderful to have a girl like Elly, past the terrible twos and terrible tens and terrible teens and be twenty and smart and able and ready to take the world in her hands. "Why can't I do something," she'd asked, the same question he kept asking himself.

Those and other random thoughts drifted through his mind as she talked, and before long he felt another idea poke itself into his internal monologue. It was muddled at first, but started to take form as she went on. Preposterous, a voice said. It would infuriate everyone, be completely misunderstood.

But why, another voice answered, because she reminds you of Philippa?

No, stupid, the first voice said, that has nothing to do with it.

He waited for her to stop. "If you're looking for a place to stay," he said, as casually as he could, "there's plenty of room at my house. You would be welcome."

There was a pause. Then: "Thank you. That is very nice. I doubt that Mrs. McKnight would want that."

"Mrs. McKnight is gone."

She looked straight into his eyes and took a little breath. She didn't respond at first. After a moment, her eyes dropped to her hands and she remained like that, not moving, barely breathing. He could almost see the connections in her brain firing.

Chapter 13

He took the morning newspaper out of its recyclable plastic bag, laid it out on the kitchen table and glanced at the headline.

TRUMP VISITS CDC IN ATLANTA

He began reading:

Wearing a red baseball cap with the words "Keep America Great," President Trump wound up his visit to the Centers for Disease Control today with a series of comments that kept the doctors by his side struggling to keep straight faces. He began by calling Washington Gov. Jay Inslee, whose state faces the most serious virus outbreak in the nation, "a snake." Next he said he had warned California Gov. Gavin Newsome not to land an infected cruise ship standing off its shores. "I don't need to have the numbers double because of the people on that ship," he told the assembled media.

Before he was finished, Trump claimed that a test for the virus was immediately available to all who wanted it, something Dr. Anthony Fauci, the nation's lead infectious diseases expert, later said was not true. Though the virus is now present in every state and spreading rapidly, Mr. Trump said,

*"we have very low numbers. Our numbers are low-
er than just about anybody," a statement in conflict
with the data.*

He read further. A Sacramento story reported that
Governor Newsome was moving to stricter shutdown rules
to relieve the pressure on hospitals, which were overcome
with the sick and the dying. Restaurants and bars no longer
could serve customers inside. Stores and malls were limited
to 20 percent capacity, down from 25 percent. He thought of
Murph's. Could Murph's stay in business with three tables
on the sidewalk? If it shut down, would it ever reopen? And
who was Murph, anyway? If Murph shut down, where would
he find Max?

He left the newspaper open while he poured his first cup
of coffee: two of life's little pleasures, morning newspapers
and coffee. He had his own grinder and French press for
brewing, using only Ethiopian or Sumatran beans and never grinding before the water was hot. Four minutes to steep,
no more, no less. He'd never had coffee as good anywhere,
certainly not in Paris, where they serve a bitter brew called
express. Certainly not at Murph's.

He reread the lead paragraphs of the Trump story, took a
sip and sat back to think about what he'd read. It was a *Times*
story, but people would be reading the same thing in newspapers everywhere. The man insulted everyone and lied about
everything, and the nation—a good part of it at least—went
on swallowing the bilge: Climate change was a hoax, the
plague was over (though still bad in states with Democratic
governors), allies like France and Germany were enemies,
adversaries like Russia and North Korea were friends, soldiers were cowards, Democrats were traitors. Western fires

were caused by forest mismanagement by West Coast governors, all Democrats. With Trump, the nation had entered the
Orwellian world of Newspeak. Repeat any lie enough times
and it will be believed.

But not by everyone.

Why was Trump, a demagogue, believed by some people,
while others knew he was a congenital liar? Some of those
who believed knew he was lying but believed anyway because
of the "will to believe," which in psychology means you can
believe anything you set your mind to, such as the "alternative facts" of Trump jargon. He thought back to his conversation with Elly. Why didn't she swallow the lies, rejected them
to the point of rupture with her father, an academic professional who did believe them. It wasn't formal education: Elly
had only a fraction of Sam Lancaster's education. It wasn't
genetics: Elly rejected the beliefs of her parents. Demagogy,
the handmaiden of tyranny and war ("truth: the first casu-
alty of war"), works only if people swallow it. How else could
the lies of Newspeak be effective; the lies of Hitler, the lies of
Stalinists like Putin and Kim Jong-un.

Newspeak took his mind to *1984*. Winston Smith, the
protagonist, sides with the proles, those who refuse to believe the lies of Big Brother, oxymorons like "war is peace, ig-
norance is strength." If there is hope, says Smith, it lies with
the proles because "the proles stayed human." Today's proles
were young people like Elly. They saw through flimflam men
like Trump, Giuliani, and Pompeo, rejected the lies, believed
their eyes. They stayed human.

The thought cheered him, and he stood to cut a piece of
baguette and pop it in the toaster. They'd set Thursday as the
day she would move in. He'd cleaned and rearranged the guest
room, put on fresh sheets and a bright bedspread and new

towels in the bathroom. Fortunately, the guest room shared a bathroom with Nancy's room, not his. He glanced at the newspaper masthead just to make sure. Today was Thursday.

He heard a car in the driveway. It sounded familiar.

"Hallo, Andy," Nancy hailed from the hallway.

Elly had said something about late morning. But how late? Having these two women meet was not a good idea. Nancy stood a moment in the doorway, inspecting the kitchen, though she knew how fastidious he was. He wasn't sure how to greet her, a problem she solved by coming in and kissing him on the cheek. Husbands get lips; exes cheeks, though he wasn't exactly an ex. Not yet. She looked improved, certainly not the disheveled thing she'd been her last time in the kitchen.

"Just needed to pick up a few things. How are you?"

"I'm fine. How are you?"

"Very well, thank you."

"Can I get you a cup of coffee?"

"Thanks. I've had mine."

Formal, meaningless words used to cover up thoughts rather than express them. He would change that.

"How's Chuck?"

She did not flinch, held his gaze, not answering straightaway. Of course, he would have guessed where she was, and of course she wouldn't lie about it. Neither of them was a liar. How could anyone lie when it was clear how lying was poisoning the country?

"Chuck is fine." She paused. And added: "So am I."

"You're looking good."

"Thank you."

She was dressed in stylish jeans and a designer tee he hadn't seen before, hair done up, nice tan and sporty Italian shoes that looked new. And why wouldn't she be feeling better, free of the man who was weighing her down, infecting her with his existential angst. She'd exchanged doom and gloom to live in cozy denial with Chuck Collins who played bridge and danced and if he felt existential angst at all, which was doubtful, disappeared into his workshop to putter it away until cocktail and bridge time.

She acted brighter than last time, though he saw tiredness, lines at the eyes and a tan that was part make-up. Why Italian shoes? Nancy had always looked a decade younger than she was, but the decade was catching up. Wordlessly, they stared. A wave of sympathy and affection for her swept over him. Nancy was a gamer.

"Do you want to talk about things?" he asked.

"What things?"

He wondered about the counselor she was seeing. "Our new lives?"

"You have one, too?" she said. "I'm glad to hear it."

He thought of Elly's imminent arrival. At Murph's, he'd invited her to move in on the spur of the moment and if he'd expected her to turn down the invitation, she hadn't. How people took it, starting with her parents and his wife and just about everyone else including Lancaster friends and McKnight friends, was their problem. He was helping a girl out who was in a fix. But his wife's first visit home since the rupture was not the moment to get into that.

She'd turned away, but turned back when she realized she'd sounded snotty. Nancy was not snotty. "I can't stay, Andy. Too many things to do."

"Can I help you?"

"Help me?"

One more misunderstanding. "I meant with the suitcases."

"Oh, yes. I'll call down when I'm ready."

She headed upstairs, and he sat down with his cold toast and coffee, the empty feeling rolling back over him. People are in control of their lives only so far. At some point situations gather enough momentum to replace individual choice with autopilot heading straight for the cliffs. Was he really about to help his wife with her bags so she could move in with another man while he'd invited a girl young enough to be his granddaughter to take her place?

But what was he to do? Join Nancy and friends in celebrating the worst man ever to occupy the White House, a preening racist who'd lost the election by three million votes and was anointed because of a Constitutional quirk devised by Founding Fathers who were afraid of democracy? Was he to act as if nothing was wrong when the man was infecting his party no less than the plague was infecting the nation and climate change infecting the planet? Was he to allow decency to be corrupted by a rising stock portfolio and an anachronistic longing for white supremacy? As much as he wished they could get back to the life they'd shared for so many happy years in this house, it seemed beyond reach.

"What have you done to the guest room?" she called down from upstairs.

"Fixed it up a little," he called back.

"Why? You never did that before."

"Time on my hands."

Not a lie, just not the whole truth. He checked the clock. The morning was growing later. "You ready for me yet?"

"I have one suitcase packed. You can carry it down if you like."

Her voice cracked.

He was alone in the den a short time later when he heard Elly's car in the driveway. As he was passing the hall table to go outside he saw that Nancy had left her house keys. He stood staring. Frozen. The message was as clear as if she'd written him a letter.

Elly was dressed in jeans, a baby blue UCLA tee shirt and sports shoes, her short hair fluffed nicely, the first time he'd seen her when she wasn't in running clothes. He grabbed a suitcase from her car and some kind of equipment bag and minutes after carrying one woman's set of bags down was carrying a replacement woman's set back up.

Upstairs, she looked around the guest room with its fine view of the pines along Carlyle. "This is perfect. Andy, How can I thank you?"

"How did your parents take it?"

"I told them I was staying with friends. I think they were relieved. It couldn't go on as it was. They have their own lives. This is better for everyone."

"Including me. I'm not used to living alone."

"Dare I ask what happened?"

"The same thing that happened to you."

He handed her Nancy's keys.

She walked to the window to look outside. The guest room had the best view. Nancy's room was on the street and his was in back.

She turned back. *"Him?"*

"Yes. Now why don't you settle in and come down when you're ready. I'll give you a tour of the castle. By the way, what's in the strange bag?"

"My fencing equipment. I'm on the UCLA fencing team."

"How did you happen to take up fencing?"

"A guy I met."

Back in the kitchen, he rinsed the press and scooped out fresh beans to welcome his new roommate with coffee. It was a strange situation, but he felt it was going to work. Elly had an easy, understated way about her, a girl who was sure of herself but a good listener, a good combination. It did not hurt that she was attractive. She had her own car and now keys to the house and could come and go as she wanted.

He'd put the baguette back in the breadbox and took it out again. She might be hungry. It was probably a more emotional morning than she let on.

"Do I smell coffee?"

"Fresh Ethiopian beans ready to be ground. I'll start brewing when the water's hot. Meantime, let me show you the house."

They walked into the back yard where she examined the apricot tree that was just beginning to sprout buds, late like other plants in the smoky climate. Back inside, he showed her the sitting room and den/office where he worked. They glanced into the dining room with its grand table and eight chairs.

"Beautiful table."

"Solid mahogany. Handed down from great grandparents on big Pennsylvania estates. In the past, occasionally useful. These days, no."

Back in the kitchen he ground the beans, put them in the press and poured in hot water. He checked the wall clock. "Four minutes." He took out a cup for Elly and butter and milk from the fridge. He pointed to the telephone. "Phones in all the rooms, one in the kitchen."

"Land lines," she said. "Do you have a cell?"

"Nancy has the cell."

"I have a cell. I won't need your phones."

"They're here if you do. The number's written on all of them."

He poured the coffee when it was ready, set down plates, spoons and a butter knife and cut the baguette. She inhaled the coffee and took a sip. A smile spread across her face. "I don't think I've ever had coffee like this."

"Better than Murph's."

She smiled. "I'm happy to be here, Andy. Thank you again."

"I'm happy to have you. If I don't have someone to talk to I'll start talking to myself, which they say is not good."

"Yes. I've run out of people to talk to. Do you know how many friends I've lost?"

"Tell me."

"My best friend, Connie Morrison, a sorority sister—I'm a Delta Gamma—she's a born-again Christian, loves Trump."

"Trump's no Christian."

"Doesn't matter. He's pro-life."

"Only recently."

"Doesn't matter." She delicately buttered a slice of baguette. "Connie was proselytizing in the House until they made her stop, trying to convince the girls that Trump was sent here to do away with abortion."

"Sent here?"

"You know how they think."

"Abortion is legal according to the Supreme Court."

"Ruth Bader Ginsburg has cancer."

"Abortion laws are state laws."

She ate as though she'd skipped breakfast.

"For Connie, it's abortion. For some others, it's race. They want to return to the days when UCLA was a white school."

"Except for sports, of course."

"Of course. For others, it's money. Most of the girls come from wealthy families. For one girl, Natalia, whose parents are immigrants, it's Trump's wall, which she loves. Such hypocrisy."

"What about boys?"

She shook her head. "I don't have a boyfriend, if that's what you mean. There is one guy, the one who got me into fencing. You'll meet him, I'm sure. He hates Trump as much as we do. He was a baby when his parents came here from Mexico. His dad, also a fencer, a really fine, funny man who liked to dress up as Zorro, taught science at Santa Monica College. When the parents returned to Mexico, Gustavo—Gus Teruel—the son, stayed on with relatives. He graduated from Santa Monica High and is at USC on a scholarship. Potential Olympic fencer."

She stopped, not sure she wanted to go on about Gus.

"And?" he asked.

"They're trying to deport him to a country he left at two years old. He may need a hideout before long."

"Go underground—like Zorro."

She smiled. "Like me."

Chapter 14

As long as he remembered, the *Los Angeles Times* had been downtown at First and Spring. It was there before he was born and still there when he went to work at the *Times* in 1990. The building was as much a downtown fixture, and nearly as magnificent, as Los Angeles City Hall, built across from it on the other side of First Street during the Depression and an iconic symbol of law and order since the days of *Dragnet*.

The *Times* was still there when he retired at age sixty-five, and he dropped in from time to time to see his former colleagues and have lunch with them in the upstairs restaurant. But the Chandlers, who'd owned the newspaper during most of the twentieth century, tired of the game, and before the century was over a new generation of cousins and in-laws decided they would rather clip coupons than work. They sold out to a Chicago real estate guy who stripped the paper and sold to a hedge fund, which stripped it some more before selling to a billionaire who moved it to El Segundo, a town near the airport known mainly for its oil refinery, the second one built in California by Standard Oil, thus the name. The newspaper was on life support. Already it was impossible to find newsstands in the city.

He'd never visited the El Segundo site, thought he never would, but after reading the paper one morning, he called Russ Posner, an old editorial page colleague, and asked if he could drop by. What caught his attention was a full page of letters to the editor from readers who said they intended to vote for Trump in November.

The wheels of his newspaper mind, idle for so long, had begun to grind.

Trump won barely a third of the 2016 vote in the nation-state of California and surely would do no better in 2020. He was not welcome anywhere on the West Coast, and certainly not in Los Angeles. The *Times* opposed him in 2016, and its editorial page and letters page had since been highly critical of his actions and policies. To see a full page of letters backing him was unique, editors stating that his supporters should have their day. Okay, they paid for subscriptions, too. The page carried ten letters. There would be more that weren't published, and Andy wanted to see them all. Understanding how any Californian could support such a freak was the first step to doing something about it.

The El Segundo building bore no resemblance to the monument on First and Spring. Abutting a freeway, it was plain glass and frame panels with all the elegance of your local Best Western. Even Posner, once a jolly, engaging type, seemed thin and dreary, like he'd been down-sized along with the newspaper. The page of Trump letters, he told his visitor, had been prompted by an op-ed piece predicting that Trump, despite a national approval rating in the low forties, would win the November election with more votes than he received in 2016. Far from supporters being sick of him, the op-ed author promised they would stand by him. The polls were wrong once. They would be wrong again.

Andy took down no names. He was not interested in the writers, but in their arguments, explanations of how people could support a man so vain and vile and whose pro-Putin, anti-NATO policies, to give them a generous name, were so disastrous. By seeing into the minds of Trump supporters he hoped to better understand people like the Godfreys, Sam and Patricia Lancaster, Chuck Collins, Nancy's bridge and country club friends, Nancy herself.

The *Times* had received thirty-nine letters in response to the op-ed. Thirteen agreed with the author. As this was to be a page exclusively representing Trump supporters, the *Times* printed the best ten. He read each letter, noting the writer's arguments in a notebook. His interest was personal, not professional. He was losing his wife over Trump; families and friends across the country were splitting up over the man. Ten letters was hardly a scientific sampling, but ought to provide clues about the writers' thinking. He wrote down their arguments as they were written, as a stenographer would have done. On the drive home, he let the ideas swirl in his brain. Throw a pebble into the pool of the mind, the Zen masters say, and watch the ripples.

Elly's car was gone when he got home, as it had been earlier that morning, as it had been the night before. It was already a week since she'd moved in, and the days had come and gone smoothly. She was a neat, polite, discreet young woman, an easy person to live with. They'd had a few meals together, but generally were on different schedules and came and went separately. When they were together in the kitchen, he enjoyed her company. She was remarkably well-informed, always bringing something to the conversation, always listening to what he had to say. If she brought vivacious young Philippa Grey to mind, he pushed the thought away. He came to understand that Gustavo Teruel was more than just a fencing friend. She asked if she could bring him over at some point, and he said of course she could. He didn't ask if she'd been in touch with her parents. Surely there'd been some communication. No parents, however in thrall of a cultist like Trump, would give up a daughter like Elly.

Before setting to work on the letters, he went to the kitchen to make a sandwich, checking the fridge to see if shopping was needed. Because of their different ages, he'd thought shopping might be a problem, but it wasn't: the top shelf was hers, the bottom his, the middle shelf and produce bins were shared. The middle shelf was packed with things they both ate: cheese, yogurt, milk, juices, tuna, eggs, hummus and various condiments. On those occasions when they'd both been home for dinner, they'd done simple meals: omelets, salads, ham, baguette and the like. He kept his case of Lavau Côte du Rhône in the nearby wine closet.

Nourished, he went into the den. Researchers had done studies of the effect on voters of Trump's "alternative facts," that is, his lies, but he'd never paid them much attention. People stupid enough to believe what Orwell called "doublethink"—the blatant falsifying of reality—were not taken seriously in his newspaper mind. Suddenly, though, doublethink had gotten personal. It was dividing friends and families. It had cost him his wife.

The ten letters printed by the *Times* used the same handful of arguments. Four writers conceded that while they disliked Trump personally, they thought his policies benefitted the nation. Three even praised his handling of the plague, which was crazy since he spent his time denying it. On each page, next to the writers' arguments, he left room for refutations once he'd done his research. After working for a while, he sat back a moment wondering why he was doing this. He was no longer a writer or editor, had no place to publish or post his conclusions. Maybe it was to prove he was not crazy or paranoid. Maybe because he had to do something beyond complaining, needed to get back into action. Philippa's last letter had gotten under his skin. *Travail: opium unique.*

The policies cited as reasons for supporting Trump were: the stock market, abortion, tax cuts, deficits, budgets, small government, immigration. None mentioned climate change, the destruction of the planet. Only a few mentioned the virus. All were angry and several alluded to saving the country for "ordinary Americans." With 80 percent of Trump supporters white, it was not hard to understand who "un-ordinary" Americans might be. The letters were contradictory, vapid and selfish, infuriating as a whole. He stretched out on the daybed to try to forget them, telling himself not to fall asleep.

At the Paris *Herald Tribune* the sports editor was a chain-smoking, beer-drinking ex-pat from Chicago named Byron Hallsberg. Hallsberg was a red-bearded Viking with a vicious sense of humor and a pretty Irish wife named Jenn. Byron and Andy were friends, and Andy relieved him on the sports desk from time to time when Hallsberg disappeared with Jenn on what he called assignment. To what he assigned himself, no one knew for it produced no stories. He'd been in Paris forever, spoke fluent French that nobody understood and knew everyone in the sports world because to get your name in the *Herald Tribune* meant that everyone who mattered in Europe and more than a few in America would see it. Artie Schwartz, the editor, was happy to leave him alone. Hallsberg knew what he was doing. He knew Paris like few Americans did, better than anyone else at the newspaper.

Learning that his occasional replacement was a swimmer, Hallsberg invited him one weekend to accompany Jenn and him to their latest discovery, les Étangs d'Hollande, a series of finger lakes hidden deep in the Rambouillet Forest. Canalized three centuries earlier by Louis XIV to carry water to his Versailles Palace, les Étangs were a well-kept secret, even from Guide Michelin. Reached in an hour if you knew all the little roads that crisscrossed the giant forest between Rambouillet and Versailles, the lakes had a small beach, a cozy café, and a square mile to swim in. Once Andy found it, he drove out whenever he could. He'd taken his wife once, but Claire disliked sun, water and, most of all, exercise.

Since arriving in Paris, he'd driven a VW bug of countless owners and miles, parking it each day at the Austin-Morris garage next to the newspaper on the rue de Berri. Going for his car one late July evening, he'd found the garage owner, a man named Maurice, waiting for him by a nifty white Porsche parked next to his bug. Maurice wore a puzzled look. "Why did I do it?" he asked, as much to himself as to Andy. He'd taken the car on a trade-in that day, he explained, but with Paris ready to empty for its annual August decampment, this beautiful car was going to sit idly in his garage for at least two months. Maurice was ready to do a deal.

Maurice's story of a widow unloading her dead husband's killer Porsche for a gentler Mini Morris sounded suspicious, but proved true. Andy checked the tires, the mileage, drove down the Champs, around Place de la Concorde, up and around the Arc de Triomphe, back to the garage and offered to help Maurice out. After some perfunctory negotiating, they agreed on a price of 7,000 francs, a ridiculously low price for a Porsche SC with 22,000 kilometers. He threw the VW into the deal and raced his Porsche around Paris that night. The next day, a Saturday, he took Philippa for the first time to the lakes of Rambouillet.

The Germans have a phrase to describe heaven on earth: *Glücklich wie Gott in Frankreich.* Happy as God in France. Maybe that's why they invade so often. France occupies the perfect spot on the planet, a place with a matchless combination of climate, land, water, resources, and people. On one side is the cold Atlantic, looking west to Britain and the New World; on another, the warm Mediterranean looking east to Italy and Greece and south to Africa. The snowy Alps and tropical Côte d'Azur are separated by only 200 miles. Even the mountains favor France, the Pyrenees sloping gently into rich verdant countryside on the French side, dropping sharply into arid barrenness in Spain.

In August, France empties north to south, every family finding something suitable for a month's vacation—mountains, seashore, countryside, little inns and auberges lining the routes along the way. History is everywhere in museums, castles, cathedrals, battlefields, aqueducts, ruins. France is, in effect, one giant museum. The French people are as varied as their land, northerners tending more to the industrious Frankish side of the heritage; southerners to the more leisurely Gauls. To the West, in Normandy and Brittany, the seafaring, warrior races.

Hallsberg and Jenn were at the lakes that day. It was a mid-summer scorcher, the kind of weather the French call a *canicule,* one he might have spent swimming in the Deligny, a floating swimming pool on the Seine, and enjoying Paris as it emptied of people. But he had a new car and a new girlfriend and so off they went to Rambouillet. He swam a mile in the lake before rejoining Philippa on the beach. Wearing a black bikini, she lay immobile on her back on a yellow beach towel, covers on her eyes to protect from sun and oglers. He sat down beside her in the shade of a beach umbrella to reflect on his extremely good fortune.

"She must be your sister or your cousin because I know she isn't your wife."

Philippa did not move. Hallsberg had snuck up. He had come to Andy's wedding and knew the girl in the black bikini on the yellow towel was not the one he had married. Still, it was no excuse for such an outrageously rude comment. Andy was ready with something equally rude, when he saw Philippa remove her eye covers, sit up and reply to this complete stranger, "I am certainly none of the above."

Then she started laughing, a deliciously sexy, provocative laugh because of the way the curves of her body undulated inside their two tiny black straps.

Hallsberg was stunned into embarrassed silence. The red-bearded old lecher had wanted to be nasty, and the mystery girl took it as a joke. He cast a final ogle over his shoulder as Jenn came up to lead him away. On the way home that evening they stopped at an auberge for dinner and then slipped into the woods to make love under the Rambouillet pines. *Glücklich wie Gott in Frankreich.*

The dream, in full color, awakened him with a start, sending him halfway off the daybed. It was not Philippa between those two tiny black straps. It was Elly.

Zen seeks to discipline the mind, to make it its own master. When unwelcome thoughts bubble up from the unconscious, you will them away. Sleep, because the will is not there to challenge it, becomes the unconquerable realm of the unconscious.

To sleep, to dream, is always a risk.

Chapter 15

His room was pitch black and the house deathly still as he lay in bed the next morning. Listening, he heard nothing, no street sounds, no yard sounds, not even a distant dog or siren. He had a housemate, but silence suggested she had not returned. Lying there in timelessness, he felt no urge to get up. The happiest part of a man's life, said Samuel Johnson somewhere, is what he passes lying awake in bed in the morning. Surely, Sam wasn't serious about that. We're not cats on windowsills or monks cross-legged in the zendo. We need action. He needed to find Max Erbsenhaut.

The thought of Johnson took his mind to the work of the day before: the trip to El Segundo followed by three hours of surfing the internet and making notes. Tedious, drudge work. Grub Street, Johnson called it. Yes, it would have taken longer without the internet. He'd have had to wait until today, drive to the Santa Monica Public Library and spend hours going through catalogs and stacks.

But what better way to spend time than in a library? Surely better than lying in bed in the morning. One day he would do a balance sheet on the internet just as he was doing on the *Times'* letters. On the plus side, speed, thoroughness, and efficiency; on the negative, far outweighing the other in his mind, the dehumanizing isolation, the unconscionable irresponsibility of social media sites in fueling the psychoticism of young Americans, and the threat to democracy in the hands of congenital liars like Trump.

He loved all libraries, particularly the Los Angeles and Santa Monica public libraries. In the old days, every newspaper had its own library and morgue, places crammed with clippings and photos dating back to its beginning, every folder double-filed under subject and writer or photographer, shelves of research books covering every conceivable subject, row upon row of stacks, thick tomes like "Facts on File" and "Who's Who" going back decades, not to mention *Roget's, Bartlett's*, atlases, phonebooks, maps, and dictionaries. Research was personal, enjoyable, and stimulating. Librarians tend to be good human beings. Libraries create good social feelings. Internet surfing does not.

With a dozen bookcases spread over six rooms on two floors, his own house was a library, not as useful as it might be because it took too long to find what he wanted. Nancy had promised to organize it, but Nancy was gone. He had books in foreign languages, books out of print, manuscripts not found in libraries or on the internet. The main point of the internet balance sheet would be to show that however smug we are about our magnificent new technology, things did get done in the old days. It took a little longer but was a good way to spend time, to spend life. Sam Johnson wrote the first complete dictionary of the English language—40,000 words with 114,000 quotations—in longhand in his London house on Gough Street with only a few humble Scots to aid him in research. He had no public libraries, no newspaper libraries, no internet, only his own eyes, own hand, own books. He created a masterpiece that is still a joy to read. There will never be an internet masterpiece.

Downstairs, he brought in the newspaper and leafed through it. The plague had dropped from killing 2,000 Americans daily in April to under 1,000 in June, but was shooting up again as the weather warmed. Trump said it would die out when colder weather arrived, but the doctors said, no, that viruses love cold weather. They feared the worst for the fall and the winter, 3,000 or even 4,000 people dying daily. Scientists had begun talking about mutations. How ironic, he thought, if Trump was defeated in November by the virus he denied.

Restless, annoyed with himself, he needed people, ideas, conversation, not sitting alone reading the newspaper and fretting over a task he'd assigned himself and had no desire to resume. He needed to find Max. Where was Elly when he needed her? He would pick his way down Alta, never a clean street, to 15th, cross to Wilshire and work his way back up to Murph's.

Max was already there when he arrived, seated at a side-walk table. "All business is now transacted on the sidewalk," he said. "Please join me."

Agnes, masked, nodded to him from the doorway. Inside appeared empty. "The usual?"

"With a three-minute egg, please."

"Coming up."

He sat down on a slat-backed chair that didn't look too steady. "Reminds me of Paris," he said, thinking of a few sidewalk cafes.

"I don't know Paris," said Max.

"You never went back to Europe."

"No desire."

"Curiosity?"

"I'm not a traveler."

"You made it to New York from Ukraine."

"Involuntary."

"New York to Santa Monica."

"Health."

Agnes brought the pot and a bagel and filled his cup. "Egg's coming."

"Who's Murph?" he asked her.

Behind her mask he detected what might be a smile. Holding the pot, one arm akimbo, she stood staring at him. With chignon, apron, order pad, pencil, and stubby black shoes, she looked born to waitressing. But there had been a past, he could tell.

"You tell him, Max."

"Agnes is Murph," he said when she was gone.

"Agnes?"

"There was a Murph."

"Left her this place?"

"In a way."

He stared at Agnes when she returned with egg, spoon, salt and pepper shakers. Max talked in riddles, but Agnes might tell it straight. "Max says you're Murph."

She smiled and patted Max on the shoulder. "Max, you are such a dear."

Max smiled back looked down Wilshire. Agnes departed.

Explanations for another day.

"Missed you a few days there," Andy said.

"My other work."

"Which is?"

"I'll take you some day."

"To do what?"

"See the set-up."

"What set-up?"

"Maybe you'd like it. What can you do?"

"I can clean streets."

Max smiled. "What else?"

"Right now I'm working on a balance sheet."

"So you're good with books?"

"Not those kinds of books."

"You talk a good game, Mr. Son of a Knight. I see possibilities." He stood. "Now if you'll excuse me, I have to go. I have other work."

Laying down some money, off he went, leaving Andy again to ponder his infuriating elusiveness. He did not look forward to returning to the drudgery of his balance sheet, but at least it was better than just talking a good game. First Philippa, now Max, the insults were accumulating. A refill seemed a good idea. He motioned to Agnes.

"Max is always rushing off," he said. "Where does he go? What does he do?"

She'd finished pouring and stood back, better to see him. "Why don't you ask him?"

"I did. He says something about his other work—wants me to see the set-up."

"I would take him up on that. You might get something out of it."

"Doing what?"

"You really don't know, do you? Well, I'll leave that up to him. Just don't get the idea that he's some old eccentric who just cleans the streets. Max is a mensch."

. . .

Elly's red Honda was in the driveway when he got home. He liked the idea of having a young woman in the house. He heard voices, heard the name Trump.

They were on the living room couch behind the coffee table with the marble Buddha. Politely, they stood as he entered.

"Andy, this is my friend, Gustavo Teruel."

He was a slender, handsome Latino of medium height, probably a few years older than Elly. His father played Zorro, he remembered, but the son would do just as well. Not hard to imagine him with cape and sword. Only needed the pencil mustache.

"Happy to meet you, sir," Gustavo said as they nodded to each other, carefully avoiding shaking hands. "Elly sings your praises."

"And I hers. Sit down, please, no formalities."

"We had fencing practice yesterday," she said. "I stayed with Gustavo's aunt and uncle. I would have called but hadn't taken down your number."

He liked the decorum as much as the apology. "We haven't established house rules yet," he said, smiling. They all sat down. "In any case, since I did worry briefly, I appreciate your concern. Could I make you some coffee? Or perhaps tea?"

She glanced at Gus, then shook her head. "Thanks, but no. We've had lunch."

"Elly tells me that you have a scholarship to USC."

"Post-grad in physiology. One more year." His English had no accent.

"If he makes it," she said.

He nodded. "There's litigation."

"Agents show up on your doorstep like the Gestapo," said Elly, "put you on the next plane to somewhere. *I've* spent more time in Mexico than Gus."

"One learns to change address from time to time," he said, softly.

Listening, Andy thought of two immigration cases he'd read about in his letters' research, letters the *Times* hadn't printed: A Mexican couple moves here with a two-year-old. The infant grows up as American as any of us, with friends, schools, and scholarships, no clue he's not as legal as anyone else. Twenty years later agents knock on the door and he is deported to a country he doesn't know. A second Mexican couple arrives as tourists, the wife gives birth, and the couple returns to Mexico two days later with an American citizen baby. Twenty years earns you nothing; two days makes you an American. Few countries have such unjust systems, which is why the Obama Administration sought to change it with the DACA program. The Republican Senate refused.

"I gather that your aunt and uncle are safe?" Andy said.

"They are naturalized Americans, yes, just as I hope to be."

"Do the agents know you're living with them?"

"I think they do, yes."

"You're welcome to stay here, if it's all right with Elly."

"That's very kind," he said, "but I don't think it's necessary."

"Did I hear the name Trump as I came in?"

They looked at each other, and Elly answered: "We're trying to decide what to do. There aren't any classes right now, so everyone has time. We have meetings with friends that go nowhere. We want to get involved but don't know how. We won't let this man be re-elected."

So that's why she brought Gus, he thought, hoping Andy McKnight might have ideas, might have a plan to help defeat Trump. He needed a moment to think. "I'm going to make a pot of coffee. Maybe you'll change your minds when you smell it."

Too much coffee, he knew, but it was a social thing. He set out three cups, sugar and milk on a tray and waited for the press to do its work. He checked the clock. He had four minutes to decide what to say. He thought of Max's comment to him: Mr. Son of a Knight talks a good game. It stung, no question, but what did Mr. Pea Skin do beside clean streets? Some other work that he was mysterious about just as he was mysterious about everything. He'd tried to get him to talk about the moral collapse of Europe, but Max had to leave. He tried to get him to talk about the moral collapse of America. Max had to leave again.

Back in the living room he set the tray down next to Buddha and poured. As he was sitting down, the doorbell rang.

"I hoped you'd be home," Nancy said at the door. "I was at the hairdresser's and took a chance." Her hair was in an updo as it usually was when she'd been at the hairdresser on San Vicente. "They called at the last minute and said to come in. They're closing tomorrow for two weeks under the new restrictions."

She looked good, much better than before, and his heart gave a little jump. Who controls the heart? "Come in. I have guests."

"Oh, sorry, I'll come back."

"It's still your house, Nancy. Please come in."

"Hi Mrs. McKnight," Elly said as they walked back to the living room. "This is my friend Gustavo Teruel."

"Hello, Gustavo. Elly, I thought that was your car. How are you? How is your family?"

"Everyone's fine, thank you."

His mind was quickly considering options, above all keeping her from going upstairs. Good thing Gustavo was there. Clearly puzzled, Nancy looked from Elly to Andy and back to Elly. Then to Gustavo. Awkwardness hung as heavy as the silence.

"I just dropped by for a few things."

"Let me get you some coffee."

"Thank you, but, no, I can't stay."

"Can I get you anything from upstairs?"

"No, I just need a few things from the downstairs closet—oh, and the garage." She turned back to Elly. "How are Sam and Patricia? I haven't seen them at the club lately. Matter of fact, I don't see much of anyone at the club these days. Please give them my love."

"Yes, of course."

"So goodbye then. Nice to have met you, Gustavo. Andy, please open the garage door while I get my things from the hall closet."

Outside, he opened the garage door and waited by her car, thinking about how to answer the inevitable questions. He would not lie. He suspected that she did not need anything from the garage, just wanted to get him outside.

"*Elly Lancaster?* What's that all about," she demanded, "and who is Gustavo?"

"She's had a breakup with her parents. She's in the guest room."

"*What?* She's living here?"

"Yes."

"With Gustavo?"

"No, of course not."

"Alone with you?"

"Yes."

"Do Sam and Patricia know?"

"No idea."

"But why?"

"Like the rest of us."

"What is that supposed to mean?"

"Why did you go off to live with Chuck Collins?"

He instantly regretted it, unsure why he was so aggressive with her. They stood staring, people who'd lived together for thirty-five years under the pine trees of 22nd Street and stopped because something came between them.

"Chuck has nothing to do with it," she said, her voice rising. Suddenly she flushed, grabbing the car door, eyes flashing, lips pursing. "Don't lay this off on me, Andy."

"What I mean is that we're not the only ones he's driven apart."

"Who, Chuck?"

"You know who I mean."

"Stop it!" She was angry. Then: "Why is she here? Why with you?"

"She had no place to go."

"Is that all there is to it?"

He thought of the dream. "You're joking."

She stood staring, anger and confusion etched into her attractive face.

"So what happens now?" he asked.

"Oh Andy, I don't know. You are my husband, but the truth of the matter is that I am happy with Chuck. I was not happy here."

They were into it now. "You're happy because you're oblivious."

"We can debate who's oblivious. Dolores says ..."

"Who's Dolores?"

"My counselor. Never mind. I thought this whole thing would go away. It hasn't."

"Maybe it will in November."

"The fact is that you're not the man I married."

"*Autre temps, autre moeurs.*"

"Oh, don't use your damned French on me!" she said, face flushed.

"Other days, other ways."

"Sorry, I didn't mean to flare up. It's just so sad."

"I'll grant you that."

They couldn't hang on, couldn't let go, were afraid of saying goodbye, afraid of what was coming. She made a move to get into the car and stopped. How did one say goodbye in such circumstances? Kissing was out, shaking hands would be insulting. They stood staring at each other, two married people in love for half their lives with no idea what came next. Maybe Dolores knew. It was out of their hands.

She gathered herself, tried a smile, a brave good woman unsure what was happening to her. "I'll have to come back, Andy. I still have a ton of things here. Thirty-five years of things in my room, in my closets, my dresser, things downstairs."

He nodded. "It's your house. You found it. You made it."

Her eyes were glistening. "Yes."

"Can I be of any help?"

She didn't catch his meaning. Then: "No, Chuck has an SUV."

"He would."

She shook her head. "Relentless, aren't you? I hope you know what you're doing. There's trouble ahead if you don't."

Chapter 16

After breakfast the next day, he went into the den to finish his project. Coming down, he'd noticed Elly's door was closed, which meant, he supposed, that she'd driven Gustavo home and moved back in. He hadn't heard her return because he slept with earplugs just in case the local dogs got out early or the emergency guys came for one of his 22nd Street neighbors who hadn't made it through the night. He'd put the project off the previous day because it was drudgery, but it had to be finished. Didn't it? He hadn't spent a day listening to freeway music in El Segundo for nothing. He'd read the letters and noted the arguments: stronger economy, ending abortion, more tax cuts, blocking aliens, etc. etc. It was time to refute them.

He stared at the empty sheet of Microsoft Word for some time, considering how to approach this. He'd thought of adjoining columns: one for the writers' points, one for his refutations. He didn't like that. He thought of sequential paragraphs. He liked that even less. He had an organizational problem, something he wasn't used to as a writer. He'd left some coffee in the press and returned to the kitchen to warm it up. Back at the computer, his brain refused to function and his fingers to move. The coffee, usually so effective, had done nothing.

Finally, he understood.

This was make-work, feckless drudge, the idea of someone with nothing better to do. The people showing up at

Trump rallies with their MAGA hats and Hooters' faces didn't care about tax cuts and deficits, small governments and big militaries. They shared Trump's hates and wallowed in his lies. They were a coliseum crowd come for blood sport. Maybe a few *Times'* readers cared enough about policy to write letters to the editor, but the Southerners and Midwesterners who worshiped him did so because he was an outrageous huckster who fed their primitivism: build a wall, isolate and divide the nation, destroy opponents, wreck institutions and above all—ABOVE ALL—make America WHITE again.

They trusted this repulsive charlatan who pretended to be a Christian, who denounced science and medicine, who promised the plague would disappear by miracle, who held rallies that infected thousands. They believed climate change was a hoax so they could go on driving SUVs, digging for oil, mining the coal that turned the air black and fracking for plastic; they supported a narcissist with a psychotic lust to defile everything, a hustler who'd lied and cheated his way into schools, "won" an election he'd lost by three million votes and used the power of social media and the perverted hacks of Murdoch's news empire to appeal to the basest instincts of race and greed.

The *Times'* letters were irrelevant. Refuting Trump's "policies" was blowing in the wind, not action but an excuse for inaction. Elly and Gus hadn't come here to talk about tax cuts and small government but about how Trump was destroying the moral and social fiber of the nation and cheering a planet on fire. Their friends agreed with them. "We won't let this man be re-elected," she'd said. They'd come to him because they thought Andy McKnight could do something beyond talk a good game. These kids meant business.

The adults were to blame, not just the crazy MAGAs but ordinary people who don't know any better. Rich, amoral television celebrities appeal to people who read supermarket scandal sheets and watch Fox News to escape from drab lives. But fraud and glitz had never carried anyone to the presidency before. Behind the pompadour and ego was a hollow man. The question was how so many millions of people could be in thrall of a person who so obviously lacked the qualities of leadership—virtue, wisdom, knowledge, experience, judiciousness and, if we want to take Lincoln as the best example, humility and humor.

Trump had none of it, and the people voted for him anyway, not a majority, he would never win that, but enough to win the electoral vote in our retrograde states. That's what set the election of 2016 apart from any other. We've had good presidents and bad ones, but when before had we ever done *that?* What comparison could there be? The Germans knew what Hitler was—he never hid it—but Hitler was not elected. He was appointed and then staged a coup to stay in power. Would Trump stage a coup if he was defeated? Was such a thing possible in America?

He closed the computer and went back to the kitchen. Elly would soon be down so he might as well make a new pot. He got it brewing and checked the clock. Barely nine o'clock, a full summer day ahead, one that might draw him to the ocean. But for now he needed ideas. His mind went to Max. Max the enigma. What was he hiding? The story of his name was all he'd ever explained. Why was his name important? And which name? What was his "other work?" What were the "possibilities" he'd mentioned? What was he doing cleaning streets?

He heard Elly on the stairs. "Good morning," she announced cheerfully from the doorway. "I smelled the coffee from my room."

The sight of her drove the dark thoughts away. "Better than an alarm clock, no?"

"I'll have a sip, but then I'm off for a run. It's been days."

He poured her a half cup. "I'm going to the beach later if you're interested."

"I think might be."

They heard the doorbell. "No idea," he said, frowning and going to answer it.

"Hello, Sam."

"Good morning, Andy. Excuse me, but I was passing and saw Elly's car in your driveway. Is she here?"

"She is here. She's having coffee. Please come in."

Sam Lancaster looked to be what he was: a pink, plumpish, tenured, middle-aged professor on the slightly supercilious side. Except for a lack of briefcase and no glasses, he might be on his way to campus in bowtie, loafers, two-toned shirt and brown corduroy jacket. He had a full head of gray hair and matching mustache. Without knowing what he taught, one would have guessed liberal arts. Fine arts and the science profs are less meticulous in their toilets. Sam had been reasonably solid and athletic at one point, but the point had passed and he'd filled out in all the middle-age places. He was more florid than the last time he'd seen him, not a good sign. He was a libertarian and thus not wearing a mask. Libertarians believe in laissez-faire, but he'd read somewhere that, oddly, they tend to be strict parents.

Elly knew who it was, but did not come to greet him. She was leaning back against the counter when they entered the kitchen, sipping her coffee.

"Hi Dad."

Instead of greeting his daughter, embracing her, he turned to Andy. "Where's Nancy?"

"Nancy's not here."

"What do you mean, *not here*?"

Andy chose not to answer, and Sam turned back to his daughter. "We've been looking for you. We've been worried. You said you were staying with friends."

"Yes."

"What friends?"

"Here."

His voice rose another notch. "Then where is Nancy?"

"Nancy is away," said Andy.

"Where?"

Andy shook his head.

Confused, angry, losing control, Sam plunged mindlessly ahead. "You mean you two are alone in his house?"

The insinuation was unmistakable, unacceptable. Elly, face reddening, fighting to say nothing that would make things worse, stared mercilessly at her father. Andy suppressed his instincts and gazed outside at the apricot tree.

"Dad ..."

Andy didn't want to hear it. He started to leave, but Elly called him back. "Please stay, Andy."

"You call him Andy?"

"Sam, really ..."

"No, no, I want to get to the bottom of this. *What is going on?*"

Elly might want him to stay, but he did not want to be there. This was between father and daughter, and the last thing he wanted was to come between them. He'd extended a hand to Elly when she needed it. Sam Lancaster was insufferable for coming here and insinuating that his daughter had acted incorrectly. Or that he, Andy McKnight, had acted incorrectly. She'd done what she had to do and so had he. A look at his daughter's face, if he'd understood it, would have told him he'd already gone too far and ought to stop before things got out of hand. If he'd come with a thought of taking her home, it wasn't going happen. Not now. A glance at his ruddy face showed he was too far locked into indignation to see that he'd lost control.

He had to get out of the kitchen so they could talk it out, try to reconcile, just like he and Nancy needed to talk it out, try to reconcile. It was the women who'd walked out, and the women who would come back. Or not. Elly was of age. The thing that kept him from leaving the room was that Sam was close to raging. The rage was still gathering inside him, but what might he do if it got out? He did not know Sam Lancaster well enough to know if he was a man of violence. Elly looked like she could take care of herself. Time to go.

"I'll be in the living room if you want me."

A few minutes later Sam shot by, saying nothing but at least not slamming the front door. He heard Elly going upstairs. The house fell eerily silent. He returned to the kitchen to finish his coffee and newspaper. He started the crossword but found it stupid. Crosswords, which used to be witty and fun, had turned into pop trivia quizzes for millennials.

Despite his good intentions, everything he touched seemed to go wrong. Younger, he'd never felt like this, always found something new and challenging to keep going. Existential angst. What the hell did it mean anyway? Nancy's friends said he was going crazy, but it wasn't him. It was the world. That's what paranoids say, Nancy said. It's not me: it's everyone else. Maybe it was age. Maybe it was senility. Who knows what goes on in the brain when you've been using it as long as he had, never giving it a rest. He needed more cold water, more RBM3. He was old and should be puttering around his garden instead of eating his heart out over situations he couldn't do anything about.

But that was the thing, wasn't it? Maybe he could do something.

Elly looked in, dressed in running clothes. "See you later."

"How did it go?"

"He has to learn." Her face was raw, like she'd just washed it.

"Take your keys. I may be gone when you're back."

In the den he saw he had no new messages. His last message was from Philippa, and he reread it. Sunday on the rue de Passy, and she couldn't write about it without blushing. How wonderful to read something like that. It lifted him immediately. Signing off with love came easily to him now. He did love this woman, or had loved her and what was the difference? Maybe it was a half century since he'd seen her, but she was as alive in his mind as she'd been in her black bikini on the yellow towel in the green Rambouillet Forest.

Proust, an expert on memory, said that if a little dreaming is dangerous, the answer is to dream more.

Dear Philippa,

I came into my den to do some work and found I'd rather write to you. Life over here goes from one dreary mess to another, and my only salvation is to plunge back into our life in Paris. I found myself thinking the other day about the Rambouillet lakes and your black bikini. How I wish I'd had a camera. To be able to look at those pictures today might restore my faith. And the rue de Passy which makes you blush! And Avenue Niel, rue Brossolette, Place des Ternes, Champs Élysées, Place St-Ferdinand, all these streets and places we knew so well. Have you ever noticed how Paris is always defined by its addresses? People in New York or Los Angeles or London talk about going to so-and-so's house, or so-and-so's shop, but in Paris it's always, "I'm going to Avenue Bosquet or rue Vaugirard or Boulevard Richard-Lenoir," the address itself takes on the character of the people and places and it's up to you to know who or what is found there. The mere mention of the rue de Passy excites me and makes you blush. To me, it is a wonderful custom, giving the city its own personality independent of the people. I say to myself "rue de Passy" and immediately think of you. It's lovely how it works.

The rue de Berri takes me immediately to the newspaper, and the Champs Élysées takes me to Churchill's. How many times did we meet there for six o'clock "lunch" when we were both working late. You taxied over and I walked over and we had some horrible English food before racing back to work. I liked Ian, the Scots bartender who'd introduced us, liked him and of course owed him. Still do. I think he had a crush on you despite hating the English. If I liked him, I hated his food. Before meeting you, I'd never eaten a thing but peanuts in that place, but before we were done with Churchill's I'd tried most of it—bangers, Scotch egg, steak and kidney, toad-in-the-hole. How Churchill's sold that stuff in Paris I don't know. When I asked you once about haggis, you said, "don't bother." When I asked Ian he said, "Yanks don't eat pluck." Pluck, I said, what's pluck?

"Better not to know," he said. Back at the newspaper, I looked it up in the Oxford:

*"**Pluck:** the heart, liver, windpipe and lungs of a slaughtered animal, often wrapped in its stomach."*

Even for the French, who eat everything, that has to be revolting.

That's it for now. I am off to cleanse mind and body in the ocean.

Love, Andy

"Yes, with everything else that was happening, I felt he might just run away."

"So you decided to run first."

"No, it was not like that! I hurt, really hurt, couldn't sleep, couldn't eat, couldn't talk, could hardly breathe. I'd never felt like that before. I had to get away."

Dolores checked her notes. "Especially on her part, you said. So you think Andy didn't feel the same way?"

Nancy sighed. "I felt that she could persuade him."

"To leave you."

"What I'm trying to say is that Andy had already changed from anything he'd ever been; from the reasonably sociable, serious but lovable man I'd known—the man I married—into someone else. Now came this correspondence. Anything was possible."

"Why did you feel that way?"

So exasperating! She never let go. "Because of everything we've already talked about, starting with Trump." Her voice was rising. "Trump, the virus, the shootings, the fires, the lies, all of it. It wasn't fun, but I was dealing with it. Then came the letters, the *secret* letters, the letters showing he was looking for a way out. It was too much."

"A way out of what?"

"Out of our house, out of our marriage, away from me."

"You say it began with Trump."

"He was so ashamed."

"Ashamed of . . ?"

"That we could have elected him."

"And you?"

"I'm not political. It didn't bother me that much."

"With time, Andy's state of mind grew worse?"

"Worse and worse."

"And yours?"

"My concern was Andy, not Trump. People were starting to talk."

"Your friends?"

"*Our* friends. They didn't want to see him. Didn't want to be insulted anymore."

"Because they didn't feel the same way about things ... about Trump."

"Yes."

"And their investments were rising, you said."

"All of our portfolios were looking good."

"What did Andy think about that?"

"He doesn't follow the markets."

"And you do."

"Yes."

Dolores sat back, staring at a table lamp across the room, a lamp giving off a weak, yellow glow. Outside was a fine spring day, the smoke from fires in the mountains thicker than on the flatlands of 22nd Street, but not as bad as some days. Except for little slivers at the edges, whatever sun shone outside did not make it through heavy drapes on the windows. It was an old house—old stucco, old beams, old trees, old street, old Los Angeles. There was no shingle or plaque outside and no diplomas or certificates on the walls inside. Dolores had them, of course, and she included all the relevant indecipherable clinical abbreviations on her business cards. But she did not display them. Her consulting room was her salon, decorated in personal if somewhat sparer style than the typical Brentwood living room.

The salon might be spare, but there was nothing spare about Dolores. She was exotic, amply built, with layers of multicolored linens dropping to her sandals and layers of dark red hair rising high over her head. Bracelets dangled from each wrist, and around her neck hung the most beautiful jade necklace Nancy had ever seen. Even through the penumbra of the room, the translucent green stones glittered as though lighted from within.

"Let's get back to the letters. If you hadn't discovered them, do you think you would still be here?"

Nancy started and stopped. Then: "I'm … I'm … does it matter? As I said, his behavior was already unacceptable."

"The letters made it more unacceptable?"

"Of course they did. This was more than simply bizarre behavior. This was love for another woman."

Dolores paused. "So was it your reaction to the letters—not Andy's reaction to them—that made the situation intolerable. Try to imagine that you hadn't found them."

"I would have sensed something. A horrible feeling hung over the house."

"Created by Andy."

"We didn't talk anymore. The only talking he was doing was to her. Anyway, it's not that I discovered the letters. It's that they existed."

"But you were already on the point of leaving. Isn't that what you said last week?"

"Yes. Kauai had not worked for us. He couldn't get past the idea that things were happening that he couldn't do anything about."

"Did he try to do anything about them?"

"I don't know what he's up to anymore. He's mixed up with people I don't know, people who have nothing to do with our normal lives. He won't come to the club. He alienates old friends who think he's going crazy. He rants, talks to himself and now comes this fantasy romance with a woman he knew a half century ago. How is that doing anything about anything? I want him to return to normal, to what he was. It's why I'm staying with Chuck. You said you thought it was a good idea, remember?"

Dolores ignored the question. "What if there is no normal anymore?"

"What do you mean?"

"Some people think it is already too late for corrective action."

Nancy was surprised. "Is that what you think?"

"What I think is not important. Chuck, if I understand, thinks like you do."

"Chuck is normal."

"Chuck doesn't feel the same passion about things that Andy feels."

"No, he doesn't. Except for me. He loves me."

"And Andy doesn't? After thirty-five years, he has stopped loving you?"

"What does it matter if he doesn't show it?"

"Do you love Andy?"

"I love the old Andy, always did. From the first day." Nancy stared into the dark to try to see into Dolores' eyes, but they were lost in the shadows. "Can't misery kill love? Doesn't a time come when you say to yourself: I can't go on like this. It is too awful. Doesn't some kind of self-preservation kick in before it's too late?"

Dolores remained silent, playing with the green stones of her necklace, caressing them, massaging them like a Muslim with worry beads. Stones of true Burmese jadeite would be worth a fortune, Nancy thought, but would someone like Dolores wear anything fake?

At length: "Did you ever consider that your husband is afraid?"

"*Afraid?* No, Andy has never been afraid."

"Would you be willing to consider it?"

"What makes you think ..."

"Wouldn't it explain a lot of things?"

"Why would he be any more afraid than any of us?"

"I don't know. Do you?"

"We're not talking about the correspondence now, are we?"

Their chairs faced each other at no more than a few feet, but the obscurity of the room, reduced only slightly by the table lamps, concealed expressions. It was a room for verbalization, not examination.

"I want you to consider, Nancy, the idea that the correspondence may have less to do with Andy than with you; to consider that he was reacting strongly to events before the correspondence began, and that the correspondence merely provided an outlet for what he was already feeling, for the fear he was feeling, an outlet he did not previously have because you did not share his feelings. Does that make sense to you?"

"No! It sounds too much like blaming me. I did not share his feelings. How could I? I thought—everyone thought—he'd lost it, entered some parallel universe."

"You couldn't talk about it with him?"

"Talking was awful. I had to get away."

"Forgive me, Nancy," she said glancing again at her notes, "but I'm trying to separate things to understand them. You said that prior to your discovery of the letters, you were dealing with the changes in your husband. Is that correct?"

"I was dealing with them, yes. But things were near the breaking point."

"Isn't it possible that the letters didn't really change anything, that the husband you are dealing with now is the same husband you were dealing with before the correspondence, a man anguished over events? That's why you went to the islands, isn't it, which was before the correspondence began. If the technological quirk that led to your discovery of the letters hadn't happened, you would not be here with me today. The letters brought you."

"Yes, the letters brought me. But it was clear things couldn't go on as they were. Andy had entered a different world, a world that did not include me. That's why I left."

"You could not deal with your husband's fear?"

"I don't think of it as fear. I think of it as madness."

"Because that's what your friends call it?"

"It's what I call it."

"Because Andy was taking events more seriously than you and your friends took them?"

"You make it sound like we're the crazy ones."

"Not at all. It's just that we probably should consider that some people may see things more clearly than others."

"That makes us the crazy ones."

"Well ..."

"No, how can it be sane to destroy your life in a futile attempt to change what one person cannot possibly change?"

"Maybe he wants to try."

Nancy was shaking her head. "We all want to do something to get back to normal. And we *have* been doing something. For years, we've contributed money, voted for the right people, recycled, I've done volunteer work. Andy has acquired some kind of picker thing he uses to pick up trash in the neighborhood. But to risk everything in anger because you can't change the world, how can anyone consider that normal? We have one life. We try to be good citizens, good people. We try to be happy. We might give it all up to save the world, but just to rant and rave about how bad things are, what is normal about that?"

"You feel that's what he's doing?"

Nancy pulled herself up in her chair. "Dolores, please understand. I respect, Andy. He's not doing anything to make a statement. He is sincere. He feels things more than most people, certainly more than I do. You say he's afraid. I say he's brave. I've told him that. I'm not brave like he is. He's able to live on the edge, live with conflict, maybe from all those years on newspapers. I can't live like that. I need calm, compassion, routine. I've been miserable since this thing took hold of him, and, frankly, since I moved out, I feel better. I'm not ashamed of what I am. I've always tried to live my life correctly. I've discovered I'm happier living with someone else, someone trying to live normally despite all the troubles we're in. Chuck cares about things, too, just as I do. But he makes time to care for me, too."

Dolores had no answer. She could always tell when she'd gotten all she could out of a session, when her clients had revealed all they intended to. The shafts of daylight around the curtains had begun to evanesce. Outside, twilight crept down the hills. She smiled. After a moment, the women stood and walked to the door. They shook hands and said goodbye. Standing alone behind the closed door, Dolores felt unsatisfied. Her hands went to the stones of her necklace, absorbing their cool, soothing touch.

Outside, Nancy stood a moment on the porch, looking down the leafy street. She took a deep breath before starting toward her car. She'd gotten nothing from the session, even thought she'd detected a note of disapproval. She would not pay another $300 for that.

Chapter 18

When he last saw Max at Murph's, they agreed to meet outside Franklin Elementary the following Wednesday at the usual time. When the alarm rang at 6:15, he rose, shaved, dressed and started down, checking the guest room door on the way to make sure Elly was still aboard. Downstairs, he brought in the paper, made the coffee, toasted the bread and looked at the front page. The summer of 2020 was something new to scientists. Not only did fires break out in mountains and forests up and down the state, sweeping through state and national parks and ravishing the giant Sequoias and redwoods that had lived hundreds of years, but there were fires in the desert.

No one knows what caused the Dome fire, the inferno that destroyed Joshua Tree National Forest. Was it the absence of spring rains, the drying out of the desert? Was it spontaneous combustion brought on by 130-degree Mojave Desert temperature? Was it a cigarette butt? Some say its origin was a lightning bolt caused by the unstable weather. The Dome fire raged over 50,000 acres and killed over a million Joshua trees, reducing to charcoal the unique forest of this elegant plant so rare and beautiful they named a national park after it. The hottest year in recorded history had produced the highest temperature recorded on earth and destroyed a yucca desert forest believed indestructible. Trump blamed Californians for not understanding forest management.

No time for tears and anger, he had work to do. He closed the newspaper, cleaned up the kitchen, grabbed hat, mask and picker and set out down 22nd Street. He looked up at the pines as he walked, wondering how old they were and how much time they had left. It was not yet seven but already ten degrees hotter than it should have been. He smelled smoke from fires in the hills. He found Max waiting outside the empty school, and they immediately set out up Montana Avenue, Max taking the leeward side where there would be more trash. The plan was to work up to 26th and then south past Idaho to Washington and do the cross streets on the way back down.

The longitudinal avenues of Santa Monica are wider than the latitudinal streets. The avenues take more traffic and have fewer trees. The avenues get you to the streets where the people live. Because the avenues see more cars and are less residential, they accumulate more trash from pedestrians and cars. Picking trash along the avenues of Santa Monica takes time. He followed Max's directions, working up Montana and turning on 26th toward Idaho and Washington. Twenty-sixth is more of a thoroughfare than a residential street, with three lanes instead of two and a 30-mph speed-limit instead of 25. Unlike the single home streets, 26th has duplexes, multi-family residences and small apartment buildings. As a busier street, it is also trashier and takes more time to clean. They'd been busy for about an hour and had filled two bags when Max signaled a trash can on the corner of Washington and crossed to Andy's side, where they emptied their bags.

They were ready to start down Washington when Max grabbed Andy's arm and pointed back down 26th. Someone driving a black SUV had thrown a full bag of something onto the street they had just cleaned. The vehicle drove on a bit farther, parked, and they watched a large man and woman climb from the large vehicle and disappear into one of the buildings.

Holding Andy's arm tight, pinching it almost, Max looked down the street, as if in a trance. "Imagine," was all he said.

They started back where they had just been.

By the time they reached the bag, it had been flattened and scattered by several passing cars. They dodged in and out of honking traffic to pick up the litter, mostly Styrofoam containers with partially consumed food and drinks.

"I'd like to find those people," said Max.

"Impossible to know where they went," said Andy.

"Into one of these buildings, but which one?"

"You want to ring doorbells?"

"No, there's a better way."

He pulled pad and pen from his pocket and started printing in large bold letters. Finished, he handed the note to Andy. "Put this on the windshield while I flatten the tires."

FLAT TIRES ARE THE REWARD FOR FOULING THE STREETS OF SANTA MONICA
Styrofoam containers have been banned in Santa Monica for ten years.

Exciting that he would take such a risk, Andy thought, eyes sweeping the surrounding buildings for moving curtains. Max was busy uncapping the valve caps on what was a new monster Cadillac Escalante. He used the butt of his pen to let the air out of four tires, tossing the valve caps into his trash bag. If anyone saw anything, no one interfered. Maybe they'd seen the trash thrown from the car and agreed with the punishment. In any case, Max was too busy to notice.

Andy put the note on the windshield, and they retraced their steps back to Washington and began cleaning the cross streets down toward Murph's, emptying their bags in the trash cans on Wilshire.

Seating was still outside, but Murph or Agnes or Murph/ Agnes had set up umbrellas to provide relief from the sun, which was climbing higher on what would be a stiflingly hot day. They set down their equipment, took seats and waited for Agnes. Three tables with chairs had been set out, one occupied by two men in shirtsleeves and ties talking about window decorations. Max nodded to them as he sat down. Agnes came out and took their orders.

Andy was impressed. He'd taken Max for the kind of pas- sivist guru who believes that retaliation is a waste of energy and emotion, and that situations, like muddy water, clear up by themselves if left alone. It was not hard to imagine the large man and woman charging from their apartment, perhaps with reinforcements, grabbing them by their necks while they used cell phones to summon police to deal with the assault on their vehicle. How would that have gone, he wondered? Two old street men beaten up and arrested for vandalizing an offensively large black Cadillac. Max would have produced the trash from his bag to show the cops it was illegal Styrofoam. Depending on the police, they might have won the argument. But what of the broken bones? Or necks?

"You're looking mighty chipper today, Max," said Agnes when she returned with their order. "What have you been up to?"

"A little mischief," he said. "Very satisfying."

Andy glanced at him as Agnes left. Yes, he was looking chipper. "Nothing like a little retribution, eh Max?"

He sipped his coffee. "And on a street we had just cleaned."

"Excuse me for saying it, but I didn't take you for a man of direct action."

The owl's head swiveled toward him. "Sometimes no action is the best action. We call it *wu-wei*. There is a saying: 'The Way never acts but nothing is left undone.'"

"But not today."

"Not today."

"Why not today?"

"Spontaneous action also plays a role."

"When?"

"As the situation requires."

"You mentioned the Way."

"Do you know the Way?"

"Tao?"

"Tao."

"Things take care of themselves?"

"Hmm, not exactly."

"What then?"

"Indirectly. Turn your opponent's energy against him."

Eating bagels, drinking coffee, watching cars and people moving slowly along Wilshire, traffic as listless as the weather, they fell silent. Andy felt good, better than he had in some time, the enigmatic energy of this old man was breaking through his pain and lethargy. He glanced at the men at the other table as they got ready to finish their break and head back to work. They put jackets back on and masks back in place. Window decorators? Salesmen in a men's store? Computers? No, computer people don't wear jackets and ties.

Shops were being allowed to open again after being shut down for most of the spring, but for how long? The plague had taken a step back, not in defeat but to gather strength for a new attack. Scientists were talking of viral mutations adapting to defeat vaccines faster than we can develop them, a microscopic mobilization taking place out of sight in a war we might never win. Victory to the tiniest. These men still had jobs, but for how long? Who was buying suits these days? They looked to be in their early thirties. What would it be like to be in your early thirties when your life and career are just gathering steam and see nothing ahead but obstacles? When he'd been thirty there were no obstacles, just ambitions and achievements. He had the feeling that nothing the nation faced anymore was temporary. The plagues might be defeated but would leave their indelible ugliness on everything. Nothing would ever be the same. His mind drifted back to Paris, to better times, sitting with Philippa on a sidewalk watching people and cars go by. Like here. Only not.

After a while, the head swiveled toward him. "I believe my instincts about you are good ones," said Max. "You are filled with repressed energy, in search of ways to use it."

Not accustomed to volunteered comment from the old picker, Andy nodded. "You are right about that."

"Yes."

"I know others who are searching as well."

"Oh? And who would that be?"

"Some young people I've met recently."

Max's eyes, which saw you peripherally, turned toward him. "How young?"

"I believe they're called Generation Z."

Max fell silent again for some time, nodding to the two men who passed on their way back to work. At length, he wrote something on his pad and handed it across the table. He put some money down and stood up. "Could you come to this address tomorrow, say at four p.m.? It's just off Venice Boulevard."

Finally some answers.

"I'll be there."

Elly's car was in the driveway when he reached home. Strange shouts from the backyard came around to greet him. Inside, from the kitchen window, he watched two fencers practicing in the shade of the apricot tree. Enchanted, he stood watching this ancient sport that he'd seen only in movies. He'd assumed it was Elly and Gus, but the shouts told him it was two women, both fully covered in fencing gear and steel mesh masks. *"Thrust, riposte, parry, thrust!"* they shouted as they moved back and forth on a linear line, nothing like the movies where the duelists leap and bound around the castle. How strange that this medieval activity should still exist, he thought, have survived the invention of pistols and revolvers that would not allow a sword-wielder to get within ten yards of his prey. Unique athletic movements with lunges and springs, dancing almost. Quick hands, strong thighs, good eye–hand coordination.

When they stopped for a break, he poured ice water, got out a tray and headed outside. *"Formidable,"* he shouted as the girls took off their masks, giving the word its French pronunciation. He set the tray on the lawn table.

"Andy, this is my friend Suzanne Martel, from the fencing academy. Suzanne, Andy McKnight, my landlord."

He laughed at the word landlord. "How do you do, Suzanne. I enjoyed watching. You two are very good."

"Suzanne is a medalist. I'm still a beginner compared to her."

"You are not a beginner," said Suzanne, firmly. "Elly has learned this sport faster than anyone I've ever seen."

They finished off the water in a few gulps and in the hot weather lost no time getting out of their gear and down to shorts and T-shirts. Suzanne had striking red hair that she shook out before pulling it back and fixing it into a ponytail. She was a tall woman, probably a bit older than Elly, attractive in a severe way, not someone he would want to meet with a sword in her hand. They sat down on the lawn chairs.

"I hope you don't mind, Andy. Probably not too good for the grass."

"This grass, such as it is, is indestructible," he said, smiling. "So tell me, how does one get into the great sport of fencing? I don't think I've ever seen it on ESPN."

Suzanne laughed. "You mean sponsored by SUVs, beer commercials, and giant cheeseburgers?"

"For me, it was Gus," said Elly. "He took me to a competition, and I told myself I have to learn this. I'd never seen anything like it—the elegance, the athleticism, plus, of course, the swords. I had to do it." She laughed. "Talk about letting off steam."

"My father is a fencer," said Suzanne. "Like Gus's father. It seems to run in families. He always talked about *la romance de l'épée*. Frenchmen, you know."

"Raised on *The Three Musketeers*, no doubt," said Andy.

"Actually he preferred *Robin Hood*," she said, "Errol Flynn and Basil Rathbone—and *The Mark of Zorro*, Rathbone again with Tyrone Power. Great scenes, no technology, just good athletes with very good moves. Inspiring. Men fighting over women. That's why I got into it: So I could fight for myself."

Elly laughed. "I was hoping you'd be back in time," she said to Andy. "I wanted Suzanne to meet you. She shares our views on—well, you know."

He smiled at Suzanne, and she smiled back. Martel, very French, he thought, Charles Martel, who saved Europe from the Muslims. He wondered if she was French like her father or it was just her name. Slight accent, hard to tell. Rude to ask. It would come out.

"The one thing I know about fencing is that there are different styles," he said. "Which style do you do?"

"Suzanne does French style," said Elly.

"Which is ...?"

"Hands, eyes," said Suzanne, moving her hands quickly.

"I do American style," said Elly, which is more legs and movement."

"So who wins?" he said, "the French or the Americans?"

"Suzanne can beat me in any style."

"What makes someone take up fencing?"

"The challenge," said Suzanne. "Plus, it is a sport in which women hold their own with men."

"But men are bigger, faster, stronger."

"Reactions. Size and strength are not enough in fencing. I have beaten men."

"Like judo," he said, "you use your opponent's strength against him."

"Exactly. Plus, in fencing there is an intangible that dates to the time fencing was a matter of life or death."

"Which is?"

"Tell him, Suzanne."

"The killer instinct."

"If she gets really mad she'll take her button off," said Elly.

"Button?" said Andy.

"The padding on the tip of the epee that keeps us from killing each other," said Elly.

Suzanne shot a look at her friend that he could not quite decipher, annoyance, yes, at being talked about, but more: a touch of pride.

"I save that for special occasions," she said.

"You've actually done it, taken the button off?"

"Let's say I've come close a few times."

The eyes showed it. This was a girl you wanted on your side.

"Speaking of special occasions . . ," Elly said.

"Ah, yes," he said. "You two are looking for action. I should have news tomorrow."

Part Three

Chapter 19

He never went to Venice anymore. As a boy, he'd lived there, and his dad would take him to the amusement park on Venice pier and then catch the tram down the strand to the amusement park on Ocean Park pier, next to Lick Pier, where the Lawrence Welk Orchestra played in its early days. In later days, he'd gone swimming at Venice Beach but always preferred Will Rogers for swimming and Malibu for surfing. Venice became too weird, too many people hanging around not for the water. Few places in Los Angeles had changed more than Venice over the years, from a faux Venetian spa at the beginning of the twentieth century to bootleggers and brothels in the twenties, fun houses and rollercoasters in the forties, muscle-builders in the fifties, drugs and happenings in the sixties and gentrification since then. The Venice canals, places of trash and oil slicks when he was a boy, now offered villas that were twice the price of the palazzi along the canals of the other Venice, the real one.

The address Max gave him was a half mile inland in one of those nondescript neighborhoods with a real estate name no one's ever heard of. The name of Max's neighborhood was Oakwood, and he'd never heard of it. The name of the street was Electric Avenue, which he had heard of, and which meant that in earlier times the Pacific Electric trolleys had taken that route from downtown to the beaches. He drove along Electric looking for the right number, and there it was, the name embossed on a handsomely lettered, illuminated sign on the second story of a long building that looked industrial.

P.S. I LOVE YOU

Odd name, he thought. P.S. for public school, maybe? Why would Max want to meet him at a public school? There was a line outside, but they weren't students. He had to drive another block to park.

Walking back, he saw what it was. The people in line were in various stages of disrepair, down on their luck but not completely down-and-out. Maybe they'd slept in their clothes, but the clothes were decent. There must have been fifty people in line, men and women, a few children, most wearing masks of navy blue with the gold letters: P.S. They acted like people who knew each other, like students waiting for classes to begin, quiet, orderly. This was their routine. They kept their social distance, eyeing him as he passed, recognizing the stranger. The building was solid, built of sand-colored concrete, post–World War II, which was when the city population began to shoot up. Outside a heavy front door, a man in blue mask and P.S. baseball hat sat on a barstool, exchanging chatter with the people in line.

"I've got an appointment with Max."

"Pull your mask up, bub," said the man as the door was opened. He shouted something to a woman across the room, who came up, greeted him, told him Max was waiting and led him across the room into a small tent. "First, the nurse will take your temperature."

They crossed a lobby-like room, through wide doors into what was a dining room and kitchen area. The dining room had a dozen long tables with chairs on both sides. The kitchen was busy, steam rising, getting close to dinner time. He noticed closed-off vents through the ceiling. Whatever the building was now, once it was something else. Light was florescent, with no windows, typical of industrial buildings. Past the dining room, they turned down a corridor and started upstairs. The second floor had window light. Outside, he saw what looked like an army campsite with rows of small tents erected across a grassy area covering maybe an acre.

His guide took him down another corridor to an office where three people, one of them Max, sat at desks in a room decorated mostly in gray file-cabinets. It could have been part of a newspaper library in the old days, with years of clippings stored in rows of metal files. Max waved a greeting. Against one wall, looking out on the campsite area, sat a saggy couch and straight-back chairs arranged around a low table covered in papers. Against another wall was a five-gallon water dispenser atop a green stand flanked by a table with coffee equipment. Despite the old-fashioned aspect of the room, each desk had a computer.

"Come right in, Mr. Son of a Knight," Max called. "We're expecting you. These are my partners, Marge and Sylvester. Coffee is ready. You can take off your scarf. We've all been tested. We are all safe."

It was an odd feeling. Max the street-picker from Murph's presiding over an organization that looked like it fed and housed great numbers of poor and homeless people, clearly a costly operation. What *was* this place, and why had Max invited him when he clearly had no shortage of manpower? Why did Max clean streets himself instead of outfitting this army of pickers and sending them into street battle?

Marge poured coffee, and they sat around the table, Marge and Max on the couch. Marge and Sylvester didn't look any different from the people he'd seen outside. Nor did Max. Nor did he for that matter.

"So, what do you think of our little operation?" Max said.

"Little? It's like an armory. I am impressed."

"We can feed three hundred people a day."

"And we do," said Marge. "People flock to us like the swallows to Capistrano."

She was a woman of a certain age who looked like she might have been handsome before weight and age took over. She had a no-nonsense attitude that reminded him of Mrs. Plummer, his third-grade teacher at Florence Nightingale Elementary on the other side of Venice, a long time ago and a long stone's throw from Electric Avenue. Sylvester was a trim young black man with a goatee and hornrims.

Marge and Sylvester explained the routine while Max silently sipped his coffee. It was a good presentation, though Andy wondered why they would waste it on him. Sure, he would contribute money if that's what they wanted. The building was a former bakery, which explained the vents he'd seen. The tents were set up in an area once used for the flower beds of a nursery that P.S. took over along with the bakery. How did they cover operational costs for three hundred people a day, which wouldn't be cheap? Who was paying? They were modernizing, Sylvester explained, converting paper files to electronic. The two of them chattered away with a presentation they'd likely done hundreds of times but said nothing about what he really wanted to know: How could Max of Murph's be behind something on this scale?

Finished, they looked to Max, who smiled. The eyes were bright behind the rimless glasses. Past eighty he'd said about his age. He didn't seem that old, didn't look it, didn't act it.

"Andrew McKnight, I see your eyes asking why you are here, and I am going to tell you. Recall one of our meetings at Murph's. You alluded to Hitler, commented that the German opposition had not seen its error until it was too late. In response, I asked that you save that conversation for another day. First, I wanted you to see our operation and hear about it, which you have now done. You've seen some of the people who show up every day for dinner, which by the way, is always a good one. This is no soup kitchen. When you leave, you'll see every chair in the dining room occupied, with people on Electric Avenue lined up waiting their turn. These are good people. I know many of them personally, know their stories."

"Which can't compare to yours."

The interruption caused him to hesitate. Then, slowly: "Not exactly ... no."

He readjusted himself on the couch and resumed. "What we've discovered at P.S. in recent months, though we've had to cancel our daily assemblies, is that these people are frustrated and afraid. They think this nation is at a crossroads. They know the election is almost here. They have watched Trump. They know what he is. They don't want to wait, as the Germans did, until it is too late."

He looked back to his partners. "Is Trump another Hitler? No, of course not. He probably won't invade Russia three times as Hitler did, and he's probably only anti-Semitic in the sense that he hates everybody. But when thousands of mental health professionals sign a petition alleging the man has serious mental illness, we have to ask ourselves what might happen to our country if he is re-elected."

He paused for a sip of coffee. "So, with help from Marge and Sylvester, I have been looking to answer the question, what can we do—we the people of P.S.—to assure that he is not re-elected; to guarantee that we do not wake up in 2021 like the Germans did in 1933, which is to say, too late? To that question, we had, until recently, no answer. We may still have no answer, but that depends on what you have to say."

Andy sat up straight in his chair, not hiding his surprise. What was this all about?

"The people who come to P.S. cannot be mobilized to do the kinds of things that need to be done," Max went on. "The average age of our guests is somewhere in the mid-fifties, but that doesn't mean the younger ones are better off than the older. Often, it's just the opposite, and you can imagine why. Even if our little band was capable of battle, they could not undertake it because of the virus. These people are high-risk, old and vulnerable, fitting the profile of people around the world who are dying. Here, at P.S., we test them, we mask them, we social distance them. We await the vaccine they tell us is coming. The tents you see outside are individual tents. Our people are as healthy as possible given what brings them here. A few have died. Not many. We have doctors. We are very careful."

Marge walked to the coffee table, bringing the pot back and refilling the cups.

"Coffee is not the woman's job at P.S.," said Max, reading his thoughts. "We take turns. Today is Marge's turn. Now, where was I? Ah, yes. You mentioned to me the other day that you know some young people who are looking for action. Would one of them be the young lady named Elly who joined you at Murph's?"

More surprise. "How do you know about Elly?"

"Agnes keeps me informed. Agnes, by the way, is a former resident at P.S. In fact, Agnes came up with the name."

Curious and curiouser. "I wondered about the P.S."

"You should not have wondered, for you speak German. Agnes also speaks German."

It took a moment to make the connection. He began laughing.

"Ah, you see the light, Herr Son of the Knight? *Es leuchtet Ihnen ein?*"

"Yes, I see the light, Herr Pea Skin. *Es leuchtet mir ein.*"

"I objected at first. The name seemed too self-serving. 'How can it be self-serving,' Agnes said, 'if no one knows what it means?'"

"She had a point," Andy said.

"Yes."

"It is a good name. Like the song."

"Exactly. Now back to where we were. So tell me, how many of these wonderful young people are we talking about?"

"I don't know. From what Elly has said, quite a few."

"Ready for action?"

"What about wu-wei? No action."

Max smiled. "*Spontaneous* action, which is of course different."

"Of course."

"Can you bring them here?"

"What kind of spontaneous action do you have in mind?"

"Ah, for that, my friend, you must first bring them. I'll say only that from what I know about both you and Elly, it is something that should appeal to you both."

"Max, you are a sly old fox."

He smiled. "Funny you should mention fox, *Fuchs auf Deutsch*. I owe a lot to that beast."

Andy had no idea what he meant and was about to ask, but Max was on his feet. The meeting was over.

"One of the times."

"There were others?"

"I think you'd better ask her."

He got up. "I think I hear the doorbell."

They had a good palaver, and afterward he sat back and watched them go at it with their swords. No question, Suzanne was the master fencer among them. Elly had talked about Gus as an Olympic fencer, but how could he fence if he was in hiding from immigration agents? Suzanne looked to be more than Gus's equal to Andy's untrained eye, but this was just practice. Do men go all out against women? She moved like a dancer, light and quick, making his moves seem awkward. He found himself rooting for her. He was curious about the divorce. He couldn't ask her directly, but from what Elly said, Suzanne was suing her husband because he was giving away money that was hers. Hers, that is, unless there was some kind of pre-nuptial agreement.

It was an interesting situation. If he were still at the *Times*, he'd have assigned someone to look into it. Can a spouse give megabucks to a candidate that the other spouse opposes without the partner's agreement? Under California property law a marriage is a "community"; what belongs to one belongs to both. In most cases, what Bruno gave away wouldn't matter much. Direct donations to candidates are limited to a few thousand dollars. But millions can be given to Super PACS. How much of Suzanne's community property was given by her husband to a super PAC supporting a man that Suzanne detested?

He was back at P.S. the next day to tell Max what he'd learned. Dozens of students would be available for the right project. Elly would bring a few of them to P.S. as soon Max had something definite to propose.

Max brightened when hearing of Suzanne and Gustavo. "Fencers," he said. "A sport where you use your opponent's energy against him."

"Like judo."

"Wu-wei. Like the Tao."

Alone that evening, he went into the den after dinner. There was a letter.

Dear Andy,

When I don't hear from you, I worry that something has happened, but how would I know? My imagination runs away with me. I'd so like to phone you, but I don't have your number. I wonder if you'd call me if I sent you mine. I'll wait to hear from you on that. I can't say that things are much better here, though my little corner is better off than other parts of the island. But America is so out-sized that your afflictions seem so much worse. We all have the virus, but we don't all have forest fires and floods and droughts and Nero in the White House. Boris is bad enough. It will be worse for our island someday because the seas will rise and drown the cities and drive us into the mountains, but we have a bit of time left before the "tipping point" is reached. That's what experts like Attenborough are saying. We do have Boris and this horrible Brexit business, which is a national disaster, but Boris is merely ruthless, not pathological like Trump. And unlike Trump, he detests Putin. We have our racial problems, but the police don't go about killing black people, and politicians certainly don't brag about it.

Chapter 21

Patricia Lancaster was at the door the next morning as he was in the kitchen. He had not seen or heard from either parent since the morning Sam came over for the scene with his daughter. He assumed that Elly and Patricia stayed in contact by phone but wasn't sure. Mother and daughter, only child, it couldn't be easy for them. He couldn't remember the last time he'd seen Patricia, didn't think she'd been to the house before, but wouldn't swear to it. There'd been many parties over the years, and Nancy did the guest lists. Patricia was not the sort of woman who makes a strong impression. She'd brought a tote bag with her.

She looked older than she was, though it was a bit of a shock to see the degradation since he'd last seen her, whenever it was. The two families were around-the-corner neighbors, but had never really been close, though Patricia was part of Nancy's bridge and tennis group at the club. She was somewhat disproportioned, not at all like her daughter who was a triumph of physical harmony, testimony to the random genius of natural selection. Patricia had a head too big for her body and face too long and thin to be feminine. Graying hair and prominent lips. Eyes more sunken than he remembered. She had not dressed for the visit but wore a brown workout ensemble suitable for errands. She'd always reminded him of Nancy Reagan. They knew each other from the club back when he'd been younger and clubbier. She hadn't been good enough to play tennis with Sam and Elly, but held her own with the other women as he remembered.

"Elly's not down yet," he said, inviting her in. "Will you take a cup of coffee with me?"

She was composed, not the indignant dervish her husband had been. "Thank you, Andy. Would you mind if I went up instead?"

"I think she's still asleep."

"Oh, it'll be all right. Just point the way."

It was selfish, and she knew it. "I know, I shouldn't just barge in, but this is hard. She won't return my calls, and I don't know any other way."

"Sam was here, you know."

"I do know. I think that's part of the problem."

He wouldn't argue with that. They were standing in the hallway, and he saw the point in sending her up. Elly might not come down for a while, and he had no intention of going up to wake her. Patricia would be used to that.

"Just up the stairs, turn right and the guest room is the one with the door shut."

"Thank you, Andy."

Later, she came down and slipped out without a word. It was close to an hour so they'd had a long talk. Whether it was a good one, he did not know. It was a solid old stucco house, and he hadn't heard a peep from upstairs. Women whispering, not like the scene with the father. If Patricia had been the first one to come over things might have gone better. He heard her car start and back out of the driveway. He opened the door to the den in case Elly wanted to talk. He'd closed it so he didn't have to talk to Patricia. He'd had no idea what to say to her and thought he might not want to hear what she had to say to him.

Elly looked in when she was down. She'd washed her face, but the signs were still there. Still in pajamas with a light terrycloth robe on top, she said good morning and sat down on the daybed. Her hair was uncombed. She carried a teddy bear.

"Gift from Mom," she said, holding it up. "Had it since I was three." She tried a smile, but it wouldn't come. "She's leaving my father. Or rather, he's leaving. She wants me to come back. I think I probably should." She dabbed at her eyes. "All she did upstairs was cry and apologize. It is so sad."

"Yes."

"She can't stand it anymore, said that Dad is going crazy with no classes and school closed and just sits in his office all day writing tracts defending Trump that nobody reads and storms around talking to himself. He's become obsessed, and the worst part is that he knows it and won't do anything about it." She threw up her hands. "How can it be? My father was always such a sensible person."

"Trump's appeal is perverse. It works best on people with resentments."

"But what resentments could my father possibly have?"

"A Russian friend once told me that the difference between Americans and Russians was that Americans want to lift people up and Russians to bring them down. The politics of resentment. There's always something if you look hard enough."

She shook her head. "Trump is a cult figure for the uneducated. Dad is the last person to call uneducated or have anything to do with cults."

"Sometimes people have a hard time admitting they're wrong."

"That's Dad all right."

He wanted to get off the subject of Sam. "So you had a good talk?"

"At least Mom understands why I moved out. She told Dad she was going to move in with Aunt Jane in Hancock Park, but he said he was the one who should go. He convinced her.

"Where will he go?"

"Campus apartments. Lots of vacancies, apparently."

"With no classes he'll have his pick."

"She didn't like the idea of him alone in the house. He's so erratic these days." She paused. "Plus, he owns guns."

The comment hung in the air. Hardly a surprise for a libertarian. He started to say about Sam not being the type to do anything stupid, but stopped. Elly was telling him her father had changed. Something had de-routed him.

She read his mind. "Mom hid the guns."

Then: "Andy, do you think it's my fault?"

"Surely Patricia didn't ... "

"No, not at all," she said quickly, dabbing again at her eyes. "I just can't help thinking that none of it would have happened if I'd been there. Mom says it's gotten worse."

"You were only there because of the plague, you said so yourself. You can't babysit your parents all your life. Every parent has to cope with the empty nest. They were relieved when you left, you said. Moving out was best for everyone."

"They were ganging up on me."

He nodded.

"Without me they ganged up on each other."

Now the tears fell, and he pulled a box of tissues from his desk. He felt like hugging her, wondered if Patricia had hugged her. Elly had done the right thing, the only thing, and it turned out badly. "Why do you think it would have been different if you'd stayed home?"

She dried her eyes. "Maybe it wouldn't have been, but I left poor Mom to face it on her own."

"That's what marriage is."

She looked up at him suddenly. "Only it isn't, is it? That's what they say marriage is, togetherness, facing the world as a team and all that, but it isn't. Put enough pressure on it, and it falls to pieces. Look at Suzanne and Bruno."

"Look at Nancy and me."

"Mom and Dad."

"Trump delights in blood sport—as long as it's not his blood. Throw the cocks in the ring and watch the feathers fly."

"So marriage is a fraud, something that lasts only until the pressure starts."

"No, Elly, it's that you can't foresee everything. I've seen marriages withstand the worst situations—loss of children, loss of love, loss of jobs. But then comes something that is such a violation that you can't pretend anymore. To go on pretending would be a violation of something too deep, too personal."

"Of ..."

"Of who you are, the stuff that makes you *you*. To give that up you might as well die."

. . .

He'd lost his appetite. After Elly went back up, he grabbed his mask and picker and went out into the streets. He would work his way down to Murph's for breakfast, hope Max showed up at ten. They'd scheduled the first meeting at P.S. for the following week. Maybe he could get an idea of what he had up his sleeve, at least understand the sudden change in attitude. In the beginning Max wouldn't talk seriously about anything, dodging question after question, answering in monosyllables. The plague, the planet, the president, Max didn't think about those things. "The Way never acts but nothing is left undone," he'd said as if some magical yin-yang force would right the world's wrongs by itself.

Then, in a trice, he was all action.

He heard barking as he walked along toward Alta and looking up saw a blondish, mask-less middle-aged woman marching down 22ⁿᵈ heading straight at him with two disagreeable, mid-size hounds straining at their leashes. He stepped nimbly into the street after spearing a plastic bag stuck in someone's picket fence.

"What are you doing in this neighborhood?" she demanded as the dogs raised a racket.

The dogs, a breed he did not recognize, were wearing red dog hats. Looking closer, he saw the MAGA insignia on the hats. They matched the woman's hat. He did not recognize the woman, but after thirty-five years still did not know all his 22ⁿᵈ Street neighbors, who tended to come and go more frequently than they used to.

"Picking up trash."

"Is that all you're doing?"

"What else would I be doing?"

"Casing the houses, checking things out."

"Lady, I live on this street."

"No, you don't so just keep moving. We don't need bums around here."

Bums? Maybe he should start dressing better on his rounds. He was about to take off his mask and give her a piece of his mind, but she looked ready to unleash the dogs, which were barking and straining at their leashes as he crossed the street and moved on toward Alta.

He was halfway down Alta when he came upon a sack of trash, likely tossed from a car by people who lived somewhere else. As he picked it and dropped it in his bag, a light bulb went off. *Es leuchtet ihm ein,* Max would say. It was the trash bag on 26th Street that had changed Max. That bag had been his enlightenment, his satori, transforming him from a doleful man of *wu-wei* into a man of action. He'd taken the bag as a personal insult, someone deliberately fouling a street he had just cleaned. "Imagine," he'd said in disbelief, staring down the street as the criminals scampered into a nearby building. He could not allow it. Spontaneous action was required. They had to be punished.

Approaching Murph's, his thoughts switched to the mystery of Agnes. Those two had a connection beyond coffee and bagels, but what was it? She'd lived at P.S., he said, even given P.S. its name because she understood the meaning of Erbsenhaut. How was it that she spoke German, a language so remote these days that they didn't teach it anymore at renowned universities like USC. Why had she been at P.S., a place for the destitute? She was Murph, Max said, but there was a Murph before her. What kind of riddle was that? She'd overheard Elly talking about cults and devil worship and pleading for something to be done. She'd reported to Max. How was it she reported conversations at Murph's to Max?

He arrived at ten, but no sign of Max. The three tables outside were empty. The neon light in the window said closed, but the door was open. Inside he saw Agnes behind the counter, drying a glass. He stood in the doorway and called to her.

"Sorry," she said. "We're not open."

"Outside tables are OK, aren't they?"

He stepped inside, and she recognized him. "Oh, it's you. Shut the door, will you? And take off that mask. You want a cup of coffee? I'll give you a cup of coffee."

He laid down his things and took a stool. She poured two cups and set them on the counter. "Can't offer you a bagel because there aren't any. No cook either. Can't run a business with three outside tables and no cook." She set milk on the counter and slid the sugar container toward him. She stayed on her side.

"Thought I might meet Max. It's ten o'clock."

"You won't see Max for a while. He's got his other work."

His other work, yes, he knew something about that. He looked closer at Agnes. She looked sixty, but probably hadn't looked much different when she was thirty. He'd seen girls of ten who had the same faces they'd have at thirty. Sixty just added a few more lines and sags. She wore a print flowered dress that wasn't exactly a waitress's dress, but you couldn't say it wasn't either. Same chignon and stubby black shoes but no apron. He wondered how he could get her talking without seeming intrusive, the secret of every good reporter. She knew nothing more about him than that he was Max's friend. And Elly's as well. Though maybe she did. But what was there to know?

"I was at P.S. the other day," he said.

"So I hear. So you know about P.S. I Love You?"

"Max says you named it."

"Good name, no?"

"It's a song, you know."

"Of course I know."

"Gordon Jenkins version, not the Beatles."

"I know that, too."

"Not many people know that."

"I've been in town for a while."

"So I hear."

"Information flows both ways," she said.

"I'm taking some kids to P.S. next week."

"Glad to hear it."

"That your idea?"

"Now why would that be my idea?"

Because you overheard me talking to Elly, he thought of saying but didn't want to risk shutting her down. "Max says you stayed at P.S. Is that before it was P.S.?"

Her dark eyes behind the square spectacles leveled on him.

"Max told me about you, said you never stop asking questions. Nothing wrong with that as long as people feel like answering them. Well, it's no secret. Murph and me ran a little place behind where P.S. is today. Rented it from the nursery. Max came around one day to say it all had to go. Big changes coming to Electric Avenue, he said. We got talking. One thing led to another."

"To Murph's?"

"Murph was my partner. That's not my name, though. I'm Fuchs. When Max hears my name he lights up like a Christmas tree. Fuchs, he says, you know what that means? Of course I know, I said. My family came over from Germany. He starts telling me, in German, mind you with a little Yiddish thrown in, that his family owned this big fur store in New York, and that fox stoles—not mink, mind you but fox— was the money-maker and what a coincidence that he should run into a woman in Venice whose name is Fuchs."

"So he sets you and Murph up here in Santa Monica."

"It was vacant. He owned the property. Why not?"

"All because of your name."

"You might say that."

"What happened to Murph?"

"He died. Never was what you could call healthy."

"Where did the old street picker get all the money?"

"From foxes, naturally, which women in California don't wear—except in old movies."

"But why?"

"Why what?"

"Why a homeless shelter?"

"Why don't you ask him?"

"I'm asking you."

She shook her head. "Ask him."

Chapter 22

They were twelve that day, and they met in a large tented canteen area behind the main building. Max, Marge, and Sylvester were accompanied by three P.S. "regulars," as Max called them. Elly, Suzanne, and Gus brought two student friends, one from UCLA, one from USC. The young visitors knew nothing of Max or P.S., just that they were invited to a meeting where a plan of action for the coming election would be presented. The main building was buzzing before the meeting began, crowded with masked regulars understanding that something unusual was happening in their life of timeless routine.

Coffee and rolls were set out on a side table under the tent. Following a period of socializing, the twelve took their places at a long table on the grass. First-name introductions were made: Cathy and Jude were the new students; Thomas, Amy, and Leo were the P.S. delegates. Max sat at the head of the table. Everyone had been virus tested, he announced, inviting them to remove their masks if they chose. After briefly talking about the mission of P.S., he said the meeting was called because they shared a common interest: helping to remove an incompetent and dishonest president from office.

Just as Max started to talk, a tall thin man slipped under the back flap of the tent, almost under, that is, because he lost his hat in the process. Scuffling for it among the flaps, he caused some tittering, finally collaring the hat and locating a folding chair at the rear. The man stood out. In addition to a sheepish look, he wore black suit, tie, and hat. No one else was dressed anything like that. If Max had seen the man come in, and he could hardly have missed him, he made no sign of recognition.

"He could win, by hook or by crook," Max was saying. "No one should doubt it. We are already into September and need to mobilize quickly. I don't need to tell you how much is at stake. If we fail, we will be cursed by future generations until the end of time." His owl's head swiveled from side to side as he talked. The man is a mystery, thought Andy, enigmatic street picker in the morning turned philanthropist and labor organizer in the afternoon.

"You," he said, looking at the students, "represent the children of this country." Turning to face the regulars, he added: "And you, just like Marge, Sylvester, Andy, and me, represent the people responsible for Trump. If we beat him in November we will partly atone for the crime of putting him in office in the first place." Up and down the long table he looked, his strange peripheral vision taking in everyone. "I'll say one more thing before turning the meeting over to my colleague Sylvester. I don't care about costs. I am an old man and a wealthy man. The people on the other side have infinitely more money and no scruples about how they made it or spend it. My money was made the old-fashioned way, through hard work."

Thus began a long meeting in which Max and his associates described an ambitious plan for electioneering in three states—California, Nevada, and Arizona. They'd done their homework. The regulars would man phone banks installed at P.S. and be responsible for the direct mail campaign. The field work would be done by the young people.

As many as one hundred fifty would be signed up, paid and sent into eastern California, Nevada, and Arizona for "canvassing—old-fashioned door-knocking," Sylvester added with a smile. The volunteers would have maps and street addresses and lists of potential supporters, all information gleaned from public voting records. California would never go for Trump, he said, but certain inland House districts in the state could be flipped. Nevada and Arizona were critical electoral vote states. The nation's future could well be decided in those two states.

Enthusiasm from young people itching to get involved in the campaign was to be expected, but what stood out for Andy was the contempt and loathing of Trump expressed by the regulars. Max had chosen each one as representing a larger group at P.S. "Nobody would speak up for Trump," he said afterward. "I looked hard. A little conflict adds spice to the dish. But if some people at P.S. support Trump, they are not confessing."

The first regular to speak was Thomas, who identified himself as a Vietnam veteran who had the privilege to speak for all the vets at P.S. He was a large black man, unusual for P.S., where the clientele was mostly white, with a little Hispanic mixed in. "The thing is," Max later explained, "that in a city as spread out as this, people mostly fall out where they live, Latinos in East L.A., blacks in South Central, whites along the coast. If they come to Venice and we can get them off the streets, we welcome them. Most stay closer to what they know."

They were sitting on folding chairs, and the one holding Thomas looked ready to sink into the grass. Dressed in overalls and wearing an African Kufi cap, he spoke slowly and deliberately on why the vets at P.S. wanted no part of Trump.

"The man is a dirt-bag," he began, "yes, a dirt-bag. Think back on what he said about John McCain." He paused briefly to look around the table. "Commander McCain was a hero to every one of us over there, a man who endured what we all hoped we could endure if we had to. Five years in torture and solitary—*five years!* He came out a skeleton. When Trump dissed McCain; when this coward, this draft dodger who's never been in a foxhole called soldiers 'losers and suckers,' I wanted to throw up. He should have been struck dead on the spot."

Finishing, he turned to each person at the table, acknowledging the nods, finally facing Max. "The vets are with you brother, whatever you want us to do."

Somewhere between forty and sixty, Amy was a blonde and still had enough blondish strands crisscrossing her skull to prove it. Her face showed hints of the beauty she must have been, though the flesh had given way. Why don't people understand that they only get one body, Andy thought, watching her sit up straighter as Max introduced her. Why do women take better care of their clothes than the body that goes inside them? There'd been a blonde named Betty Thorpe in his Venice High School class, a girl so stunning that the day after their senior graduation party she got on a bus for Las Vegas determined to make a name for herself and return to Hollywood for a movie career. He'd danced with her grad night at the Del Mar Hotel, and she told him her plans. He'd danced that night with every girl in his class he'd ever had a crush on, but would never have dared have a crush on someone like Betty Thorpe. While she was in Vegas he went to college and into the army and to Europe and he didn't see her again until their fortieth high school reunion, back at the Del Mar, which was a club by then. He wouldn't

have recognized her without the nametag. Too many ciga-
rettes, drinks, and men. The former beauty looked like the
dissipated grandmother of some of her homelier classmates.

She didn't make it to the fiftieth reunion.

He sat staring and trying to remember why Amy made
him think of Betty Thorpe. She wasn't quite so far gone, and
she'd made an effort for this meeting with heavy lipstick, a
barrette in her thin hair and a butterfly brooch on her baby
blue sack dress. She lived in a tent and did what she could
with what was left.

"They call me Amy," she said, with a Texas drawl, "but my
real name is Amelia. I look more like an Amelia these days
than an Amy, so from now on I'm Amelia." She smiled. "Now,
as for this man we're here to talk about, the orange monster
I call him, I'm not gonna say it's all his fault—not *all* of it, we
girls still have to buy the spiel, don't we? But yeah, most of it
is his fault, and I'll tell you why. The thing is ..."

Flustered, she stopped. She'd forgotten the thing. She looked
to Max, whose calm demeanor told her not to worry, she'd find it
again. And she did. It was hard for her. And it hurt. Amelia was
dried out. Max didn't allow alcohol on the premises.

"The thing is," she said, setting her jaw and welcoming it
back, "as kids, you just don't understand. You're seventeen
or maybe twenty or even twenty-two from out on the plains
somewhere and you start in the big city with some guy. He
holds all the cards, right. You've got nothing but your body,
so you have to trust the guy. It's a fair exchange, right? And
before you know it—*this!*" She pointed at her face and looked
across into the stunned faces of Elly, Suzanne, and Cathy.
"Go ahead, take a good look. THIS!"

She stopped a moment, and her eyes went down to her
fidgeting hands on the table. "What I'm trying to say is that

without trust everything goes to hell. If guys treat you like dirt you end up in the dirt. They've got the power. We've got our bodies, that's it. And pretty soon we got nothing. We trusted the guy and got dumped. Or worse, which I won't go into. There are millions of guys like Trump, like this Hollywood guy, what's his name, who orders girls—even stars—down on their knees to do you know what. Trump is the worst. The way he looks at us and talks about us like we're trash. No wonder he's sued by so many women. Just no trust with that guy. The others follow his lead and get away with it because *he* gets away with it. They get away with it with their lies and their lawyers and their big bucks." She sniffed and stopped and turned to Max. "Thank you Max. The girls at P.S. are ready to help."

Silence. Every eye was glued on Amelia. The three young women across the table stared, maybe wondering if in fifty years—but no, impossible. Amelia looked at them and tried a little smile. Okay, maybe what she said was full of self-pity, but said in a language they all understood: Her eyes stayed dry, but when she saw approval in those three young faces, she teared up. She had scored. The tension went out of her body, and the smile spread across her tired old face.

Leo was the last of the regulars to speak. A small nervous man, he did his best to stay in control of a body that did not want to obey. He turned in his chair and pointed out to the field and said that he lived out there in row three, tent fourteen. "Been there now for over a year. Hope to move on one of these days—nothing personal, Max old buddy—you know I've been saying that since I moved in. While I'm here I'll give you whatever help I can."

He paused and then nearly jumped out of his chair. "Sorry, sorry." He sighed. "Happens to me. Tourette's. You've heard of that. Story of my life. You never know what part of your body's going to act up. Nerves have minds of their own—look, see that damn twitch there. I never know about that one. Anyway, we're not here to talk about me. What I want to say is this: Four years ago, just over four years it was, August 2016, Trump goes to South Carolina for a speech. I saw it live on TV. Sittin' in some bar in those days. There he was blasting away at the media for being fake news and corrupt and all that, and in the middle of his rant mentions a reporter named Kovaleski that he particularly doesn't like. And Trump starts doing this ..."

Leo stood up quickly and started jumping and shaking his arms and hands and twisting his neck like his head might fall off.

He heard the gasps. He'd wanted to shock and succeeded.

"Yeah, that's right. Have a good look. That's what he did."

Flushed, he sat back down, exhausted.

"Trump's making fun of Kovaleski," he went on. "I mean, really making fun of him, mocking him, ridiculing him on national TV. Serge Kovaleski it is, and I wrote him about it, and he wrote back. Turns out he's got something like Tourette's, it's not Tourette's, but it's close, makes your body act up. And so here's Trump up on the stage shaking and making faces. And you know what? The guy who was ridiculous that day is not named Kovaleski. His name is Trump, and anyone who can do something like that is the absolute scum of the earth. The good lord doesn't make people like that; they come from the devil himself. So Max I'm with you and so are the men who chose me to come to this meeting. We'll man the phones and lick the envelopes and do whatever we can to drive a stake into this vampire's heart once and for all."

Things calmed down as the young people spoke up, one by one, thanking Max and P.S. for inviting them and asking about the details of what they would be expected to do, how they would travel, where they would stay, how many would be needed.

Max said everything would be worked out at subsequent meetings once they knew how many people signed up. The first step was recruitment, and for that he had P.S. people already working on flyers and posters to be distributed on campus and at off-campus sites. He thought that fifty canvassers for each destination would be about right. They would spend October on the road with accommodations arranged by contacts that P.S. had in each area. All participants would be paid a wage still to be determined. He asked the visitors if they thought they could sign up one hundred fifty volunteers. They said they thought they could.

Arrangements were set for the next meeting the following week. Class was adjourned.

Leaving the canteen, Andy saw Max approach the man in the black suit and lead him toward the group where Elly and her friends were gathered. Why would he do that, he wondered? There were some smiles and laughs, and the man in black walked out of the tent with Suzanne and Gus. A lawyer, Andy decided. Anyone else would have dressed like the natives. Or an undertaker. A staff undertaker?

Chapter 23

Elly didn't find out the same way he did. It would have been too horrible.

She'd moved home to be with her mother, who caught the virus and was moved to Santa Monica Hospital leaving Elly quarantined alone at home. Sam Lancaster had moved into bachelor campus apartments in Westwood. The once happy Santa Monica country club family had been shredded. How did Tolstoy put it? "All happy families are alike; each unhappy family is unhappy in its own way."

But the happy Lancaster family must have been unlike other happy families because the story on the front page of the *Times* informed readers that Sam Lancaster, tenured economics professor at UCLA, had jumped off the roof of the Engineering Building the previous day. Few details were known, wrote the reporter, but Professor Lancaster reportedly was despondent over the breakup of his family. Calls to the Lancaster home went unanswered.

He sat at the breakfast table staring at the newspaper. The reporter clearly didn't know the whole story. Would he have written it had he known it? Would he have written that Sam Lancaster was despondent because the lies of a reptilian president crippled his mind, drove his daughter out of the house and helped send his wife to the hospital? That kind of hard truth doesn't get into news stories. The reporter also didn't write that the Economics Building where Sam worked wasn't high enough so Sam walked over to Engineering, the tallest building on campus. He knew where he was going, what he was doing. With Covid, nobody else would be around so he could get to the roof without being stopped. True libertarian, Sam went out on his own terms, dispirited because the Trump poison had seeped into his own happy household.

He pushed newspaper and cold coffee away, went to the phone and with unsteady hands looked up Lancaster in Nancy's telephone book and dialed the number. No answer. He thought of walking over, but the ringing telephone said don't bother. Anyway, Elly was quarantined. Would she try to see her mother at the hospital? Would they admit her? With Patricia hospitalized, Elly would have to handle the details of Sam's suicide, but how could she do it while quarantined? Suddenly, a thought crowded in. Did he play a role in Sam Lancaster's suicide? If Elly hadn't come to live with him would things have gone differently? But she had to move out, she said. If she hadn't come to 22nd Street, she would have gone somewhere else.

Wouldn't she have?

He went into the backyard and started walking circles, breathing deep to calm his nerves. That poor happy family, one a suicide, one sick maybe dying, one quarantined and desperate. He went back inside and dialed again. Still no answer. He headed out into the streets. God, what a mess. A body lying in the morgue at UCLA Medical Center waiting for someone to come for it, start making arrangements. He had to do something.

Elly's departure from 22nd Street had not created a vacancy for she'd immediately been replaced by Suzanne Martel at the instigation of Ignacio San Román, the man in black

"Why not?"

"Something about foreigners."

"How did you hook up with someone who didn't like foreigners?"

"I don't know many lawyers."

"What do you know about Iggy?"

"Quite a few articles in the *Times*. Takes hard cases. Ruthless. Tends to win."

Andy smiled. "Your type of guy."

"Exactly."

"Like Bruno?"

She sighed. "Bruno wasn't always like that. Bruno changed."

He waited to hear more about Bruno's change, but Suzanne showed no interest in talking about the man she was divorcing.

"Interesting name. Where's Iggy from?"

"His family came from Mexico."

"I hope he doesn't get deported before the trial."

"Family arrived ages ago. Before the rest of us."

"Doesn't matter how long you're here. Nobody's safe."

"You marry Trump you're safe."

He laughed.

She wore jeans and a T-shirt with crossed swords, her red hair pulled back and tied. She had gloss on her thin lips and no make-up. There was something Wonder Womanish about Suzanne, he thought, an athletic, "don't mess with me" quality, especially with the crossed swords across the chest. What does a woman like that see in a hedge-fund type like Bruno Brassard? She said he'd changed, and it was obvious what she meant: Trump brought out the worst in people, stoking hates and desires they didn't know they had.

He hadn't met Bruno, surely wouldn't, but he had his own prejudices and one of them was that there was no more useless, parasitic activity than hedge funds, private equity companies, and all the other so-called "vulture investment" banking businesses like Blackstone. Like vultures, they stripped everything they touched to the bone before discarding it and backed a cancer like Trump, one of their own, for legal protection.

From personal experience, he knew that part of the attraction in the mating of incompatible people was the exoticism. Picking friends, we choose people of common experiences, common interests. Picking spouses, attracted by the challenge and flattering ourselves that our appeal is ubiquitous, we get reckless. Only a year into his Paris marriage, he'd already understood the dynamic. Married for four years, Suzanne was just finding it out. Those four years corresponded precisely with Trump's time in office. When he'd asked Elly how someone like Suzanne could have married a man like Bruno, she'd turned the question back on him, unfairly, he thought. Nancy did not support Trump in 2016. Influenced by her country club friends, she supported him today, maybe only as a passive supporter, but an enabler, ultimately as responsible for the degradation as Schwarzman, Brassard, Sam Lancaster, Elly's sorority sisters, Nancy's clubby friends, and the MAGA dog woman. That's what hurt so much for he still loved her. They'd been seduced by a hustler, a television mountebank. They saw the damage and knew what four more years would do. They couldn't stop themselves.

Such a situation in America had only happened once before, during the Civil War, when families and friends were set against each other as viciously as soldiers on the battlefields. In normal times, people support different parties, policies and presidents and still get along. Families and friendships take priority over politics. American plurality endures because both parties are trusted: the governing party and the loyal opposition. As in any two-party system, they differ on policy, but traditionally not that much on values. In times of national crisis, they trust each other enough to come together in coalitions and unity governments.

Today was different. Trump was a corrupter of his own party's values. His own advisors, his own cabinet, didn't trust him. They'd signed on with him for personal fame and fortune and were ready to jump ship at the first sign of blood, expecting a pardon if they landed in jail. They knew they were contaminating the system. They knew Washington would need a thorough fumigation when they left. The goal was to line their pockets and get out in time.

A few days later, back under the apricot tree with Suzanne to discuss the funeral service they'd just attended, he heard a car in the driveway. For a moment he hoped it was Elly, but knew better. At Westwood cemetery, she'd thanked him for helping with arrangements and left to try to see her mother, who was out of intensive care but still bedridden at the hospital. As for the arrangements, nothing could have been simpler. A few flowers, a few people, put the urn in the ground and cover it up. Tears and condolences from those friends and family who'd come. No preacher in sight. Elly was masked and wearing dark glasses and dark clothes. Her face, what could be seen of it, was deep raw red.

He heard car doors and listened for the front doorbell. Instead, he saw Iggy San Román and Gus Teruel coming around the side of the house. Puzzled, he looked to Suzanne, who'd lost her color at the cemetery and still not regained it.

He was about to call out when Iggy put a finger to his lips. "We were followed," he said. "I lost them somewhere around Pico."

They'd finally come for Gus, Iggy informed them, which explained why neither one had been at the cemetery. Immigration agents knew Gus was staying with his family in Culver City, knew where most of the foreign students staying in California under provisions exempting them from deportation were staying. Some half million of them were in the nation, half of them in California, young people brought here as children by their parents prior to 2007. Most of these young people had never known any country but the United States. For four years Trump had sought to deport them only to be stopped by California law suits and the courts.

As November approached and he sensed how the political winds were blowing, Trump unleashed the full fury of his resentments—denying the plague, pardoning Republican criminals, opening national parks and forests to development and the oceans to oil drilling, rescinding air and water standards, firing agency and staff members who resisted him, rushing through a Supreme Court nomination before the election, attacking and undermining the Post Office, warning people not to vote by mail, ordering agents to arrest people like Gustavo Teruel, warning that the coming election would be fraudulent, ordering his supporters to take charge of polling places across the nation, threatening the survival of our democracy by refusing to commit to a peaceful transfer of power.

He even asked William Barr, the feckless attorney general, about pardoning himself and his nepotistic family just in case they should be indicted after leaving office. A wounded beast, Trump was capable of anything. Some said he would organize a mob to march on Washington to prevent Biden from taking office should he be elected. That seemed an exaggeration. No president had ever done that.

"I think Gus should stay with you for a while," the lawyer said. "Immigration knows nothing about you. This is a safe house."

The shock of protest on Gus's face told them he knew nothing of Iggy's plans. "No!" he cried. "That is totally unfair. Excuse me, Mr. McKnight, I had no idea that this is why we came here. I thought Elly would be here."

"I think it's a good idea," Andy interrupted. "You'll have to share a bathroom with Suzanne, but that shouldn't be too inconvenient. What do you think, Suzanne?"

"I don't mind if he doesn't."

"Well ..."

"I like it," said Andy, interrupting again. "A safe house to protect against Trump hit-men instead of the KGB and the Mafia. Why not?"

As Iggy left, he handed cards to all of them. "There is no way they can connect Gustavo to this house, but you never know when these guys get on the warpath. If they come around, whatever you do, don't go with them. Stall them and call me at one of the numbers on the card. I'll be here in minutes."

Chapter 24

Murph's was shut up, but Max still stashed his bike in the back. With all he had to do, somehow he still found time for his morning chores. The plan was to meet outside Franklin Elementary and go from there. As the plague surged, so did the trash, pride of community buried under addictions to plastic and Styrofoam. California did not have the highest death rates, but had the highest death totals because of its forty million population. With its large and vulnerable Hispanic population, Los Angeles was hardest hit of all, hospitals filled to over-capacity with the sick and dying.

He brought in the newspaper, had a quick cup of coffee and decided not to leave a note for Suzanne and Gus, which was too house-motherish. Besides, they knew the routine. Outside, the sun was peeking through the pines on what would have been a typical Santa Monica September day but for the smoky haze that drifted down overnight from the fires on Mount Wilson. He put on his mask, walked down 22nd to Alta, turned up to 23rd and headed for Franklin. Still a block away, he spotted Max standing in front of the school by a car. Looking closer, he saw it was a black and white Santa Monica police car. He assumed it was Santa Monica police, though they used the same cars as the Los Angeles police. Two officers stood facing Max, who was backed up to the car. A little farther on, on the sidewalk, stood a woman with two barking, middle-size dogs wearing red MAGA hats.

"What's going on?" he asked, approaching.

"Just keep moving, sir," the female officer answered through her mask.

"That's him, that's him," the dog woman was shouting. "That's the other one."

Her dogs started up at the sight of him, straining at their leashes.

"You mind showing us some ID, sir," the officer said.

She was a large woman, not the sort one likes to argue with. She seemed the officer in charge. Her partner, a slim, black man, looked about half her size.

"Good morning, Max," he said before turning back to the police officers. "Why would you ask me for an ID? I live around the corner on 22nd. I am taking a morning walk. You mind telling me what this is all about?"

"We'll ask the questions," said the male officer through his mask.

"Well, ask then."

Silent, composed, his scarf up over his lower face, Max leaned against the police car with his hands behind his back. Could he be hand-cuffed?

"Do you know this man?" the female officer asked.

"Of course I know him. He's my friend."

"We have a complaint from this woman here."

He glanced at the dog woman, who looked like she was dying to turn loose the MAGA dogs. "Would you please ask this woman to silence her dogs," he said. "There's a Santa Monica ordinance against barking dogs. You are the Santa Monica police, aren't you?"

"It's written right on the shield here, sir," said the male officer.

"So what's the complaint?" he asked.

"We've had several against two old men loitering outside Franklin School."

"Loitering?"

He looked in his book. "That's what it says."

"From this dog woman?"

"Andy," said Max gently, raising a finger to his lips behind his red bandana.

At least he was not hand-cuffed.

"Do you see this thing in my hand?" said Andy, raising his picker.

"Put your weapon on the ground!" commanded the female, her hand automatically flying to her holstered revolver.

"This is a trash picker, officer," he said loudly, activating the trigger.

The black officer took out his weapon. *"On the ground with it. NOW!"*

He dropped it beside Max's, which was already down. It was unnerving, embarrassing, comical, but he didn't know how to stop it. He'd covered incidents like this in the old days, things that start for almost no reason, escalate and become impossible to stop. The dog din was attracting some onlookers. He looked to see someone he might know but didn't know a lot of people on 23rd. The problem was, he'd done nothing wrong. Nor had Max. This was harassment instigated by the MAGA woman.

"The dogs," he shouted over the racket.

"Lady," shouted the male officer, "shut those dogs up or I'll call the pound."

"Why shouldn't they bark?" she cried back. "They're scared of these perverts."

"It's not us they're scared of," Andy called back.

"I repeat," said the female officer, ignoring the noise. "Do you know this man?"

"Of course, I know him."

"You mind telling us his name?"

He looked at Max, whose eyes said, no. Andy understood. Maybe he was thinking of the old days back in Galicia. "Why don't you ask him?"

She looked at her book. "He says his name is Pea Skin. Is that right?"

He kept a straight face. "Yes, this is Mr. Pea Skin."

"That's obviously not anyone's name. Ask him why he won't show us an ID if that's his name? We're going to take him in," she said. "And it looks like we'll have to take you in, too, for obstruction. You want to show us some ID?"

"I repeat, that is his name. Do you speak German?"

"So he's foreign? Is he illegal on top of all this?"

"On top of all what?" He glanced at Max, who remained expressionless. "Let me get this right. This woman of the barking dogs—who is also not wearing a mask and therefore is in violation of two Santa Monica ordinances that I know of—complains of two citizens who are cleaning the streets. And you're going to take us in and not her?"

The police were getting nervous. They'd been pushed into a ridiculous situation by an awful woman and didn't know how to get out of it. Max had decided not to make it easy, and Andy understood why. What right did this busybody informer woman have to accuse them of anything? He looked at the black officer, who'd at least put his weapon back in the holster. Was there something racial in this? But the policewoman, who was white, was clearly in charge. Did Max *want* to be taken in? Did he not carry an ID on him? He wouldn't have a driver's license because he rode a bike.

"Your accomplice would not show us an ID. Do *you* have an ID?"

"*My accomplice?* By what right are you stopping us from cleaning the neighborhood streets. Santa Monica only cleans its streets once a month. Do you know that? If every citizen did this do you realize that there would be no more trash?"

The female officer looked at her partner and sighed. "So you don't have an ID either."

"By what right do you have to ask me for an ID? I am a citizen cleaning my street—actually it's not my street because I live on 22nd. Imagine it was snowing and I was out here with a snow shovel instead of a picker. Would you arrest me then?"

The woman smiled: "Snowing in Santa Monica?"

He couldn't stop himself. "You know what I mean."

"We already told you," said the male officer. "We have complaints of two old men loitering outside Franklin Elementary. Are you foreign as well? You're supposed to carry an ID at all times."

"I am not," he said loudly. "This is not Russia. Not yet, at least."

"What do you mean by that, sir?"

"You know what I mean." He looked to Max again. "We are not loitering. We happen to meet here."

"Why?"

"Because it is convenient for both of us."

"Why an elementary school?"

"That's it, that's it," shouted the woman.

"Do you see any children around?" He knew his voice was rising, but couldn't stop it. "What are you insinuating? What did this MAGA woman tell you? This school has been closed for months."

"You're refusing to show us your ID?" said the woman.

"On the basis of this woman accusing us of loitering? Yes, I am. And when I come before the judge I will ask why you arrested us and not her. Have you taken down her name?"

"Don't worry. Get in the car, please."

"What about our pickers? They are state of the art."

"We'll take them, don't worry."

Andy looked at the female officer. "Are you really sure you want to do this? I can tell you now: You're going to look mighty stupid in court."

She wasn't at all sure. She looked at the male officer.

"Get in the car," he ordered.

Santa Monica City Hall is a long, white, two-story, Works Progress Administration art deco building built during the Depression. Like most WPA buildings, it is well-built and looks almost as good as the day it opened. The nearby jail-house is newer and uglier and not built in any known style but at least is more or less hidden from view by a massive freeway interchange. The jail walls are thick enough that you can't hear the freeway noise from inside, where the main sound is the clanking of doors.

Neither one of them had a cell-phone, but the police allowed Max to make a local call before they were moved to the holding area. He located Iggy San Román in Beverly Hills, and Iggy made it to the jailhouse, which he knew well, in under an hour. Two hours later they found themselves, along with various other perps, cops, lawyers and witnesses, standing in the courtroom as Judge Nathaniel Augustus Cooper entered and took the bench.

With a lined, craggy face and hair as white as the white of the flag that stood by his desk, the judge looked as Early American as his name.

"Retired," whispered Iggy. "They don't waste active judges on misdemeanors."

The other perps, whose crimes had preceded theirs, went first: domestic violence, road rage, running a stop sign, speeding, jaywalking, mostly people who could have mailed in their fines but wanted to appeal. The judge was brusque and efficient, sometimes giving ground but generally backing up the arresting officers.

Time crawled. Andy's mind drifted, occasionally coming back to the courtroom but most of the time miles and years away. Somewhere during the second hour, he happened to glance at Max, sitting next to him, motionless, silent, lost in contemplation. He thought of the question he'd asked Agnes, the one question Max seemed always to avoid.

"Ask him," Agnes had replied.

Why not? This time he couldn't get away.

The lawyers in the road rage case droned on. The accused had thrown a beer can through the window of a women's moving car, missing the woman but hitting her dog. Because of the open beer and signs it was almost empty, DUI had been added to the assault charge. The defendant's lawyer asserted that the woman provoked the incident by making an obscene gesture, something the plaintiff, a grandmother, denied she would ever do.

"Max," whispered Andy, trying to sound as casual as he could, "what made you start something like P.S.?"

The old man sat still as an oak, bandana up, eyes fixed ahead behind rimless glasses, hands motionless in the mudra position, a man existing in total tranquility, big mind, they call it in Zen, lost in the universe. He showed no inclination to answer, no sign he was aware of the question any more than he was aware of the man who'd hit the dog with the beer can.

Andy felt embarrassed. He'd had no right.

At length, just as the woman was describing her dog's extreme chagrin at being soaked in beer, the head swiveled toward him.

"Debts."

"Debts?"

No answer.

"How do you start something with debts?"

More silence. Then: "Not *with* debts. *Because* of debts."

"Debts to whom?"

"Debts to everybody."

The courtroom was nearly empty when their turn came and they moved to the front. Judge Cooper looked at the charge sheet in front of him, looked up at them, back at the charge sheet and up again.

"Would the gentleman in the red bandana ... Mr. ah, Pea Skin ... kindly lower it a moment so I can see his face."

Max pulled down the bandana and the judge's jaw fell, at least his mask did.

"Max Erbsenhaut," he demanded. "What the hell are you doing in my courtroom?"

"Haven't seen you in a while, judge," Max called back with a wave.

"Morning, judge," called Iggy San Román.

Judge Cooper listened carefully to the testimony of the officers, thanked them and dismissed them. Iggy San Román rose to refute before the officers left, but the judge waved him back down. "Not now, counselor," he said curtly. The two knew each other.

"Now, Mr. Pea Skin," he said, "you do some good work in our community so tell me this: Why did you provoke those officers?"

"I apologize, judge. They did nothing wrong. Just fine us and let us be off."

"But why, Max, *why?*"

"If you'd seen the woman, judge," intruded Andy, "you'd have your answer."

Judge Cooper shifted his gaze, showing annoyance. "Please take down your mask, Mr., ah, McKnight. You live on 22nd Street, I see. How long have you lived there?"

"Thirty-five years, judge."

"Thirty-five years and you've never been in my court before."

"No sir."

"If you had, you would know that I don't like unsolicited comments."

"Sorry, judge."

"As for your particular unsolicited comment, you needn't worry. The officers wrote the lady a ticket for public disturbance. I expect I will be seeing her about it because she always appeals. As for you two, I hope I don't see either of you again. Max, you get back and take care of your people. I'll waive the fine for you and Mr. McKnight of 22nd Street. How do you explain your behavior, Mr. McKnight?"

"I apologize as well, judge. The heat of the moment."

"Hmm. You two are old enough to know better. I should ..."

He stopped to reflect.

"Never mind. Case dismissed. And don't pick fights with my officers again."

Chapter 25

He was in his den the next morning, settling in for a full day of writing to friends and former colleagues, everyone in the newspaper business he'd kept ties with, stirring them up for the coming fight. The plan was for most of the election work to be done at P.S., but he did not intend to sit by while others did all the work. Thanks to Max, Elly and friends, and the MAGA dog woman he was motivated as he hadn't been in years. *Travail: opium unique.* Activity would help drive away the misery gnawing at him for so long.

He'd just settled in when the doorbell rang. Suzanne and Gus were in the back practicing fencing, and he was expecting no one. His first reaction was that it was Immigration, and he pulled Iggy San Román's card from the desk drawer and put it in his pocket before going to the door. He had no desire for another scene with the law.

His wife stood there with Chuck Collins a few steps behind, his mammoth SUV squatting in the driveway like an invading tank. She had an uncertain look on her face, which he understood. How would he feel knocking on the door and asking admittance to the house he'd lived in for thirty-five years? Nancy had not only lived in this house, but found it and decorated it and once told him she loved it more than any other place she'd ever known.

Seeing her was growing more painful.

She tried cheerfulness, but it didn't really work. She'd phoned but couldn't reach him because he was always out and didn't have a mobile phone and if she left messages he didn't see them or answer them, she wasn't sure. He couldn't argue. He'd shut off the message beeper ages ago and sometimes forgot to check the blinking light, which was hard to see anyway in the daylight. He didn't explain why he hadn't been home. She didn't need to know he'd been in jail. So here she was at the door with her sheepish-looking paramour a few steps behind. They'd come to collect things she needed from her closets upstairs.

He felt for Chuck, who with his saggy-assed overalls and mostly bald head looked more like a moving-van guy who shouldn't be doing this work anymore than a former friend now shacked up with his ex-friend's wife. He briefly considered helping them, deciding the situation was pathetic enough without adding to it. With his two young roommates in the back, he fortunately had no introductions to make. He watched as Nancy led Chuck upstairs to her bedroom, an incongruous thought, then headed back to the den, closing the door out of habit, then opening it again in case she wanted something. He cast a quick look around for anything she might claim. There was nothing. It was his room.

Almost immediately he heard a cry from upstairs, and not a gentle one. He was being summoned. He'd forgotten that the last time she'd been over no one was lodged in her bedroom. With Gus's arrival, Suzanne had moved into her room, leaving Gus in the guest room, the two lodgers agreeing that Nancy's room was more suitable for a woman.

"What is this?" she demanded as he arrived.

It was the first time he'd looked into the room since the switch was made, and, yes, it appeared that Suzanne was not as fastidious as Elly, most likely because as Mrs. Brassard in Beverly Hills she'd had servants. Not that the room was in total disorder, but neither was it maintained with the military order that Nancy liked. Plus, certain changes had been made, natural enough since Nancy had been gone a while and the room had had two new lodgers. Suzanne apparently did not like Nancy's bedspread set, which was on a chair in the corner. Nor was she a meticulous bed-maker.

"I thought Elly was in the guest room," Nancy said.

"Actually, Elly moved back home," he said, wondering if she'd heard about Patricia and Sam. She hadn't been at the funeral. He looked at poor Chuck Collins standing under the pink lace valances and looking out on 22nd Street. For some reason he reminded him of Oliver Hardy, sans Hitler mustache. If Chuck had said a word since arriving, he'd missed it.

"*So?*"

"You asked about Elly."

"Whose things are these?"

"This is Suzanne's stuff."

"Who is Suzanne?"

"A friend of Elly's."

"And why is she here?"

"It's a longish story."

"In *my* bedroom?"

"You want it back?"

"NO! I don't want it back."

Her tone sharpened his own. "Then don't be a dog in the manger."

"Dog in the … Andy, what dog? WHAT IS THE MATTER WITH YOU?"

He shouldn't have said it because it was gratuitous and she probably didn't get it anyway, but the situation was awful.

Chuck had started to turn around and stopped, turning back to 22nd Street.

"I thought you wanted to know about Suzanne."

She turned around to take a deep breath. It was something he'd always admired about her, the ability in the midst of a meltdown to stop herself, catch herself, count to ten, breathe deeply or whatever and calm down. She had a little bit of what Max had. Not a lot of it, but some. He, Andy, had none of it, but he admired it.

"Are you running a boarding house?"

"We call it a safe house."

"A what . . ?"

"It's another longish story."

"Spare me. So if Suzanne or whatever her name is has to stay here, why isn't she in the guest room? Why is she in this room, my room—or rather my old room?"

"Why would you care?"

Finally, Chuck turned. "Andy, I don't think ..."

"As it happens, Suzanne *was* in the guest room, but then Gus arrived, and they decided the guest room was better for him. More neutral, he said. You remember Gus, don't you. He's the young man who was here with Elly the last time you dropped in."

Speechless, she glared. Silenced, Chuck turned back to the window.

"I'll go back down now unless you need me for something."

"Thank you, Andy. I don't think so."

Back downstairs, he sat at his computer listening while Chuck made several trips carrying things out to his vehicle. He was feeling empty and stupid, knew he hadn't said the right things upstairs but didn't know how to act with her anymore.

After a while she came in and sat down on the daybed. She'd calmed down. They were finished. "I think I have everything now."

He turned to face her, not trying to hide his anguish. He saw the same thing in her face. They understood. They'd reached the end.

"Tell me," he said, "how could we have lived together so many years, never with an argument, at least not one I remember, and now this?"

She didn't answer, was fighting for composure. Then: "Andy, I don't want to live alone. Do you?"

His voice fell to a whisper. "Then why did you leave?"

Now the anger broke through. "Because I *was* living alone. You weren't here anymore."

It took a moment to find an answer. She was right and he knew it and couldn't do anything about it. "And I'm still not here, am I, not entirely. To be honest, I'm not anywhere. I am adrift, lost at sea. Trying to find land again."

She dropped her eyes. The old Nancy. "I'd like to help. I can't."

"Yes."

"I know you're taking things hard," she said. "But I have my own life to live. Do you understand?"

"I do now."

"I can't carry the world on my shoulders like you do. I admire you for it, but I'm not strong enough. I'm not you."

"Don't give me credit I don't deserve."

"Do *you* want to live alone?"

"Of course not," he said, softly. "I wish you'd come back."

Slowly, she shook her head. "I can't. Those last few months in this house were too awful."

"It's your house, you know. Do you want me to move out?"

"This is no time to talk about the house."

"No."

She stood up. "I must go now."

He stood to face her, wanting to keep her from leaving, wanting to pretend none of this had ever happened, wanting to get back to normal again.

But there was no normal anymore.

She kissed his cheek. "Goodbye Andy."

"Goodbye, honey."

She left, and he stood alone in the empty house, her house, *their* house, the poison of misery seeping through his mind and his body. He tried to drive it away, but couldn't. He thought of Sam Lancaster, understanding. Lost, he closed the door and lay down on the daybed, eventually falling into a stupor, dreaming he was on the edge of a high building, dreaming he was jumping.

Late that night, his two roommates off to their beds after a dinner of giant pizza, salad, and a bottle of Lavau Côte du Rhône, which he mostly drank, he was back in his den. Philippa was on his mind. With its mixture of Brexit, tipping points and the island in the Bois de Boulogne, her last letter had been so exquisitely perfect that he needed to respond while he had it in mind. When had he ever been able to reminisce about things like that with Nancy?

Chuck Collins. *Oh, God!*

He stared at the blank screen for some time. So much on his mind, but how to order it? Be spontaneous, says the Tao, but nothing came. He wanted badly to escape back into the arms of the pretty girl waiting for him in her gypsy flat on the Avenue Niel, greeting her with the bottle of Brouilly or Saint-Amour he'd brought up from Chez Jules.

But none of it was there anymore. Yes, he kept it alive with memory and correspondence, as she did, but the thought that they could somehow return to it was delusional. Philippa's nineteenth-century sandstone Haussmann building was likely replaced by some anonymous glass and panel office building. Chez Jules would be a Monoprix or Mini-Mart or a place to buy the latest mobile phone. Philippa was a granny, and he, Andy McKnight, was no longer a dashing young foreign correspondent but an old crank who got into street arguments with MAGA dog women and had been abandoned by his second wife.

Reality was not a Paris that was no longer there, but the collapsing Trump world he awakened to every day. Max and Elly had brought him back, and he would throw himself into their election project with all his energy. They would run Trump out of Washington and put him in prison. They would flip Arizona and Nevada, give the Congress back to decent people and start undoing the damage done to planet and nation by Trump's gang of grifters. He sensed the same determination across the nation: people who'd seen the nation ripped apart, who'd seen spouses, families and friends set against each other; people who'd never before been involved in politics mobilizing and shouting from the rooftops: "I'm mad as hell and I'm not going to take it anymore."

If they failed, failed collectively as a nation, he would move to New Zealand. He would write Jack Ferraro, and he would write Philippa. She would come with him. She was as sick of Britain's collapse into disease, resentment, and corruption as he was sick of it in America. If Trump somehow won again; if people were lying to pollsters because they were ashamed to admit they would vote for him; if he got another four years despite losing another election because of our deformed Constitution, the lesson was clear: the nation was permanently stained. If that happened, he would leave. He would write Philippa and tell her his plan. She would come with him to a place that the Trumps of the world could not reach.

Wouldn't she?

Of course she wouldn't. How many children and grand-children did she have? He'd have to check her early letters, but it seemed there were a lot of them. For all the love and remembrances in her letters, she would never give up the comfortable life she'd created over the past half century in her little corner of the British island in a delusional attempt to recreate something that no longer existed.

He dared not even ask.

But he would go himself, and he would continue writing her from Down Under. He loved their correspondence. The thing about it was that they were no longer old people living in a defiled world when they wrote. They were back in their twenties again, feeling the excitement of making love in the afternoon on the rue de Passy, maybe in the same building, the same room—who knows, maybe even the same bed— where the Marquise de Merteuil and the Vicomte de Valmont engaged in their exquisite debauchery.

Finally, his fingers started moving.

Dear Philippa,

# # #

Acknowledgments

To all those writerly friends and colleagues who helped and advised me over the years, especially those in San Francisco, Honolulu, New York, Paris, and Los Angeles. Above all, to Sanford Zalburg, erstwhile city editor of the *Honolulu Advertiser*, who (eventually) paid this young reporter the ultimate compliment: "Enfin, the twit is learning how to write tersely."

James Oliver Goldsborough is a 40-year newspaper veteran, working for the *New York Herald Tribune, International Herald Tribune, Newsweek Magazine, Toronto Star* and various western newspapers. He was an Edward R. Murrow fellow at the Council on Foreign Relations. His first book, *Rebel Europe*, was written for the Carnegie Endowment for International Peace, and praised by the *Los Angeles Times* reviewer as "the most important book I have read in years." He has also written *Misfortunes of Wealth, The Paris Herald, Waiting for Uncle John,* and *Blood and Oranges.* He attended UCLA. He has lived in Santa Monica. He now lives in San Diego.